Penguin Crime Fiction
Editor: Julian Symons
The Mushroom Cave

Robert Jay Rosenblum was born in New York in 1938
and educated at Brandeis and Yale universities. After
graduating, he became an assistant producer of feature
films, working on such films as Peter Brook's adaptation
of *Lord of the Flies* by William Golding. He has also
been a song and script writer and had a musical play
produced in New York, off Broadway, in 1968.
Accepting an offer from a London theatrical agent, he
and his wife, who is a Ph.D. research chemist, came to
England in 1968, where they have remained ever since.
His first publication was *Eight Lights*, a history of the
Maccabean struggle. *The Mushroom Cave* is his first
novel.

Robert Rosenblum

The Mushroom Cave

Penguin Books

Penguin Books Ltd,
Harmondsworth, Middlesex, England
Penguin Books Inc.,
7110 Ambassador Road, Baltimore,
Maryland 21207, U.S.A.
Penguin Books Australia Ltd,
Ringwood, Victoria, Australia
Penguin Books Canada Limited,
41 Steelcase Road West,
Markham, Ontario, Canada L3R 1B4
Penguin Books (N.Z.) Ltd,
182–190 Wairau Road, Auckland 10, New Zealand

First published in the United States for
the Crime Club by Doubleday & Company, Inc.,
Garden City, New York, 1973
Published in Great Britain by Victor Gollancz 1974
Published in Penguin Books 1976

Printed in the United States of America by
The Colonial Press, Inc., Clinton, Massachusetts
Set in Linotype Times

For Connie

Delivery

The bow of the boat slapped into the waves. The waves hit back. Water showered over the gunwales and seeped between the planks of the scummy deck, launching a shimmering flotilla of old fish scales. The lank young man in the stern watched a spider swept up by the swashing torrent try to climb onto one of the tiny silver rafts. One black hairy leg took hold, the other legs flailed searchingly. A new rush of water washed away the kicking pebble.

End of show. The young man pushed his long black hair away from his eyes and squinted at the shoreline – another in a long series of efforts to find a landmark that would coincide with the chart spread open in his lap. Straining to see into the brightening day had given him a headache. As the sun rose higher, the shading of distant hills was bleached to a flat green ribbon fringing the silver sheet of sky. Now the topographic profile he saw no longer jibed with any of the chart information. But he could not give up searching for some recognizable hump of land, some distinctive jutting of the coast. There must be a basis for the vital decision: whether to proceed farther north, or veer into the circling pattern.

He looked at his watch. Slightly more than two hours out. Perhaps he had already left the relative safety of Turkish waters. Without a speed indicator it was impossible to make a reliable estimate of the distance he had travelled. Yet he accepted the uncertainty as a necessary annoyance. A speed indicator – any navigation aids – would look suspiciously out of place aboard this rotting tub. The hull of this boat was no longer the mere creation of men; it was a full collaboration with Nature, at the midpoint between artifact and driftwood.

Under the circumstances, the young man didn't begrudge the old fishing boat its lack of conveniences. The crippled timbers, leaky seams, frayed ropes and rusted fittings went nicely with the story he would have to tell in the event of a boarding by a Russian patrol. The presence of any device to assist navigation would cast serious doubt on his excuses. In any case, there was little advantage to pinpoint positioning. Russian patrol boats were not unknown to ignore the niceties of naval jurisdiction when their suspicions were sufficiently aroused. His instructions had prepared him for the possibility of being towed into a Red port. To protect his credibility, only a cheap pocket compass and a large 'General Chart of the Black Sea (Western Shore)' had been provided. For good measure, the chart had been 'aged'. The word applied to artificially antiqued furniture, 'distressed' would be more suitable. Faded, tattered, stained, worn through at the creases, the chart was practically useless. But it made him smile. He imagined some Ph.D. in a spotless white smock, working in an underground room applying seven years of higher education to the specific end of chemically creating this useless item. It was a dividend of the mission to think of those smug college boys working, after all, for him.

It helped to think of the dividends, to dilute his growing irritation. Shit, they could have allowed him binoculars; plenty of tourists carried them. Trying to match the pale distant landscape against the ruined chart was impossible without binoculars.

He gave up. By the best guesswork – two hours' travelling at an estimated speed of six knots – he had arrived at the designated rendezvous area, opposite the Russian-Turkish border. He leaned lightly on the tiller and arced the boat towards open sea. Holding in a circle of approximately a two-mile radius would keep the boat visible across enough open water to compensate for a fairly large error in his figuring.

The wire of pain behind his eyes was ratcheted tighter by the unrelenting hammer of the single-cylinder motor. In the beginning, everything about the engine had seemed comical. It was housed in a low square hut set amidships, fifteen feet forward of the stern. When he had first seen the boat at the dock, he had assumed this was a cabin. But inside he had found room for nothing but the engine. No place to stand, no floor. The throttle control was a length of thick hemp cord which reached to the stern, from where the boat was steered. He had soon learned that the motor was finicky; tying off the cord had precipitated a coughing fit in the carburettor, followed by a stall. Life could be sustained in the engine only by constant adjustments of the throttle. He had to keep hold of the string every moment, and after two hours his fingers were stiff and aching. And the motor's sound, the rackety fart which had once amused him as a comment on the mission, had turned cruel.

He dipped his free hand over the side into the slicing cold water, then pressed the chilled fingers to his forehead. Closing his eyes, he leaned back against the transom. The cool darkness soothed him, the soundless gallop in his head faded away. In a black daydream, a tiny automobile drove spotlighted to the centre of a red ring and released a stampede of clowns, then raced away making a fat funny noise.

He opened his eyes. The boat had come almost full circle. He had been dozing for twenty, perhaps thirty, minutes. The day to which he woke was darker, a cloud lingering over the sun like a drooping lid over a brutish eye. The duller grey light brushed in some shadings on the landscape, and he tried again to match the conformation of steep forested hillsides with some line on the chart.

His scanning caught something – far to the north, a pin-prick chip at the base of a green wall. It was too distant to define its lines or dimensions, detect any movement. But possibly because it had the look of a defect in the natural vista, possibly by some exclusively modern human instinct, he felt it was a city.

The three-hundred-mile crescent covered by the chart included four cities. Rize was the only one in Turkish territory, and that was thirty miles south of the village where he had boarded the boat. Of the three Russian cities – Sochi, Suklumi, and Batumi – the latter was closest to Turkey. It must be this he had just glimpsed at one o'clock off the starboard bow. In daylight the city would not be visible unless he had already penetrated Russian waters.

He shoved the tiller over hard. The boat shuddered violently as it came about, butted through the waves. A swell of fear, a belief in the deadly consequences of intrigue, was followed by a blanketing calm, as if his emotions had pitched up and settled into a trough along with the boat. What could happen at worst? The adventure would change shape. Instead of the quick climactic thrill – package tumbling through the air, caught in his hands, motors roaring away to opposite horizons – there would be the slow tense battle against official doubts, the sly drawn-out exchanges of interrogation, a few thoughtful days in a cell, a ride to the border between silent men. But a prolonged testing of his nerve would bring compensations, a greater return of pride, a greater proof of courage than could be earned from an afternoon's cruise in an old boat.

He heard it then, the low confident hum of high power gliding furtively across the water. His eyes were pulled by the sound to a point inland, diagonally off his port bow. But he saw nothing there. The ghost motor danced in and out of silence, getting louder until there was no more silence but the rising and sinking volumes of a sustained rumble. A gusting wind started to stipple the sea with whitecaps. He searched the frothing sea for one that was different, water peeling back from a knifing bow. It seemed a long, long time before he could pick it out. Heading north, heading for him.

His contact? Or a patrol?

He breathed deeply, trying to dispel the panic.

Anger took its place. Why hadn't they allowed him binoculars? He could have read the land, known when he had gone too far. And right now he'd know what was coming his way.

A fine time to argue the point. There was nothing to do now but wait. He let go of the throttle string, and the motor stalled.

Clippings

Keeper had found the rocking chair on the beach in front of his house. It was a plainly carpentered cane-backed rocker of the kind that line the porches of ramshackle resort hotels frequented by elderly people. There had been a few of these hotels farther along the beach, but they had been pulled down as the area was developed for expensive beach houses. The rocking chair was probably one of many that the wreckers had left to be carried off by the sea. Battered and bleached but still usable, this one had survived.

There was something knowing about the sea, Keeper thought, that it had cast up the chair when it did, at a moment when he felt so appropriately old and used up. He had settled into the house only the night before, straight from the duplex apartment willingly surrendered in the separation agreement. Waking the next morning, he had seen the chair from his bedroom window lying overturned on the sand. He had gone immediately, still wearing his pyjamas, to put the chair upright and bolster its sagging joints by hammering in a few nails. Then he had sat down in it for the rest of the day.

Two weeks later he was still spending most of every day in the rocker. The routine underwent few variations. There were days when he changed out of his pyjamas or shaved. Also, as the phone began to ring more frequently, he started carrying the chair from where he had found it, placing it far from the house so that the prevailing wind would carry sounds away. Otherwise, he was not disturbed. The beach belonged to him for three hundred yards either side of the house. All the land was fenced off except where stone breakwaters divided separately owned tracts of beach. In summer, Keeper might have been distracted by his neighbours, rich families of waterskiers. But it was October, the other houses were empty; deserted and cold, the beach was in season only for brooding romantics and the hopelessly lonely.

He rocked back and forth for endless hours, a purposeless pendulum in a timeless clock. Ideas and memories, wishes and regrets rolled into consciousness and receded like a surf breaking. And perhaps when the tide was out, thought Keeper, one truth would be left behind, stranded like a piece of driftwood on the beach. Then he would know what had gone wrong.

A multimillion-dollar electronics corporation he had started twenty-five years ago in his parents' garage on a G.I. loan. The beautiful wife, prized for the youth against which he tested himself. They had been his. He had not merely lost them, but had given them up. Why? He knew that he had stopped caring, had surrendered the battles to keep them; he knew that much. But not why, why it had all ceased to matter.

Sometimes he wondered if the decline of will had begun with divorcing his first wife. A more solid, sympathetic woman than his second wife, she had helped him through the difficult early years of his business, had given him a son. Did the end of a first love leave a flaw that could grow into a crack, widen and spread until everything else was undermined?

Sometimes he decided it was simply age: getting older.

Yet Keeper was only fifty-one and looked ten years younger. His tall figure unstooped, still lean, his brown hair barely brushed with grey, gave him an appearance of the kind that constitutes a corporate asset. In the days when he had been building his company, his look as well as his arguments had been good for bank loans. He was not overly handsome; that might have put the bankers off, fearing their money would be siphoned into playboy pursuits. Keeper had a face that inspired confidence. The blue eyes over strong cheekbones slanted subtly in a way that suggested shrewdness, but stopping short of the foxy cunning that often escalated to recklessness. His thin-lipped mouth would have looked cruel on some men. Coupled with a strong jaw, it gave Keeper an air of self-contained assurance.

He understood these effects, had relied on them. But lately, whenever seeing himself in a mirror, he perceived a weakening. He didn't project the same solidity, couldn't. Something from

which he had drawn strength, something outside himself, had
let him down. He didn't know who or what it was that had
sustained him; he only knew the faith was gone.

'Jack!'

A man stood on the sun deck of Keeper's house, shouting
into the wind.

Keeper didn't answer, didn't turn, but continued gazing over
the ocean into the sinking sun. During the past two weeks his
name had been shouted many times. Wives, lawyers, bankers,
whores – he had relived arguments with all of them in his mind.
This was just one more faint cry out of memory.

'Hey, Jack . . . !' The cry was louder.

Now Keeper looked behind him and saw Andrew Fall slog-
ging his way through the sand. Fall was his lawyer, a harried
and humourless man who looked perpetually hot and rumpled,
even on winter days. Objective enough to realistically assess his
own professional ability, Fall never forgot that he owed his
success to two coincidences. The first was that he had been
drafted in 1944 into the same Marine unit as Jack Keeper; the
second was that, having decided to wash in a jungle stream, he
had moved to hang his helmet on a tree branch at the same
moment a Jap sniper had taken a shot at the man sitting under
the branch. The helmet had stopped a bullet that would otherwise have ended inside Jack Keeper's head. It was hardly a
heroic gesture, but Keeper had always been grateful, and after
the war had given Fall the best part of his legal work.

'Jack . . .' Fall hovered out of breath. He skimmed the sweat
off his wide balding brow with one finger.

'How did you get in?' Keeper said.

'Broke a window.' The lawyer's hands flapped the air apologetically. 'Well, I saw the lights through the window . . . clothes
lying all over the floor . . .' He took off one shoe and concentrated on pouring sand out of the heel. 'Christ, Jack. I've been
calling for days and you don't answer. To be honest, I thought
I might find you lying on the bathroom floor with your throat
cut.'

'You worry too much. Go home, Andrew.'

Standing heronlike, Fall tried to put the shoe back on. But
his portly body was difficult to balance on one leg. For almost

a minute he hopped in a circle, chasing his own raised foot, until at last his hands caught it and replaced the shoe.

His embarrassment would have lasted longer, but then Fall realized that Keeper wasn't amused, hadn't even been watching.

'Jack, I can help. Let's talk about it.'

'Talk.' A rush of air came through Keeper's nostrils, the tail end of a hopeless gut laugh. 'I've been talking too damn much for too damn long. Talked myself in and out of two marriages. That was half of it anyway, talking them into bed – the wives, and the ones they screamed about. And businesses. I talked while the money came and went, deals turned hot and cold. That's enough talking.'

Fall moved around in front of Keeper. A long-reaching wash from the incoming tide slipped under his shoes and he jumped onto the sand, a small crazy ballet step.

'Have you been reading the papers, Jack?' Fall asked quietly.

'I haven't been doing a goddam thing.'

'Then you don't know,' the lawyer murmured. 'You don't even know.'

Keeper said nothing. Silent, swaying, he seemed to be asleep. Fall thought twice about delivering the news without being asked for it. But finally he did:

'The Russians have your son.'

Keeper gave no sign that he had heard.

Fall stood by the chair another minute, then walked back to the house.

Stretched out on a sofa facing the television set, Fall woke to a pictureless picture, the cathode dawn of early morning. Sitting up, he kneaded a cramp in his shoulder.

Keeper was at the end of the couch, watching the moving fuzz of light.

'What time is it?' Fall asked, rubbing his face.

'Ten minutes past "The Star-spangled Banner".' Keeper left the couch, switched on a lamp, and turned off the TV. Then he plumped himself back down. 'All right, Andrew. Let's talk.'

Working to dredge the facts out of his sleep-logged brain, Fall remembered the clippings in his attaché case. He picked it up from beside the couch, brought out a sheaf of papers and handed it to Keeper.

The cuttings were generally small, none from the front page, no bold glaring headlines. The only picture of Roy was on top. It was an old one, dating from his days as a popular debutante escort; Roy was in tuxedo, his black hair neatly combed. More recently, Keeper knew, the hair had grown long, shaggy; and the black-tie uniform had been traded in for equally constant blue denims.

The caption under the picture read: HELD BY RUSSIANS.

Keeper gazed at the photograph for a long moment, then turned to a ragged square of newsprint underneath. This was a wire-service story, no by-line. The headline said: MILLIONAIRE'S SON ACCUSED OF SPYING; the dateline was 'BATUMI, Adzhar Autonomous Soviet Socialist Republic, U.S.S.R., 17 October.' The story filled two short columns.

Russian authorities have announced the arrest of Roy Keeper, a 22-year-old American taken yesterday from a boat off the coast of this Caucasian oil port. The Russian communiqué said Keeper would be charged with 'espionage and ideological subversion'. The U.S. State Department issued a statement that no further information is available as official contact has not yet been established in the matter of Mr Keeper's arrest. The charge of ideological subversion has been used in the past to denote anti-Communist propaganda activities. Accordingly, it is felt that the espionage charge does not involve the exchange of top-secret material. However, distribution or handling of illegal propaganda is a serious offence under Russian law. If convicted, Keeper could draw an extremely harsh sentence from the court. In previous cases dealing with related activities, sentences of up to ten years' imprisonment have been meted out; a provision for hard labour would be mandatory.

Neither of Keeper's divorced parents could be reached for comment. The father is Jack Keeper, who founded Forge Industries. Starting with a small electronics company, he built Forge into one of the first corporate conglomerates. He was forced out of the company three years ago after overextending merger operations, which caused the stock to decline severely in value. The shares, of which Mr Keeper retains a large bloc on a nonvoting basis, have since reached new highs.

Mrs Susan Keeper, mother of the accused, was said to be en

route from her home in Wyoming to Washington, where she will be briefed and advised by government agencies.

Keeper flipped to the next story. The same sparse facts had been recorded, freshened by the comment of an unidentified State Department spokesman that ideological subversion potentially included 'anything from tuning in Voice of America on a transistor to snatching Mrs Brezhnev's grocery list'. Keeper dropped the packet of cuttings to the floor, leaving the rest unread. As they fell, the containing paper clip came off and they scattered over the floor around Keeper's feet.

'Of course, it must be a trumped-up thing,' Fall said quickly. 'Not the first time they've grabbed a wayward tourist.' He knelt to rummage inside his attaché case, open on the floor. 'I have some statistics –'

'Never mind, Andy.'

Fall hesitated. 'I don't suppose they're any help, really. I just grabbed whatever I could.'

Keeper moved to the long marble ledge where the liquor bottles stood. His slippered feet shuffled through the litter of clippings, dragging them under his feet, tearing a couple.

'What are you going to do, Jack?'

Keeper's hand fiddled in the ice bucket, now filled with tepid water. 'Did you fill the trays again?' he grumbled.

'No. Sorry.' Fall started collecting the papers scattered on the floor. He had all except one pinned under the heel of Keeper's slipper, when Keeper spoke again:

'Haven't seen the kid in eight years, Andy. Did you remember that? I'd forgotten how old he was until I read it just now.' He looked down at Fall. 'So why always come to me? You can't expect me to care. He's only one of the things that happened between me and a wife I used to know. She's content to leave it that way. She never sends you to me, right? So why tell me every time the kid is hit with a drugs charge, or knocks up some co-ed virgin? You want the fix money again, all right. Put him down for a grant from that tax-gimmick foundation you've got my name on. But I don't want to know any more.'

Fall could smell and feel the air rising out of Keeper's stomach, warm and rancid. He'd never before smelled anything wafting from Keeper but the delicate and expensive – cologne

16

from silver bottles, old brandies. This was something else, the authentic aroma of crack-up. It was senseless to have come, Fall realized. Hoisting himself onto the couch, he crammed the clippings into the fanned-out pockets of his attaché case. 'I thought it was my job to let you know,' he said, closing the latches with a determined snap. He stood up. 'What you do about it is your business.'

Keeper was standing at the terrace doors, staring into the night. He said nothing.

Fall yawned. At this hour the two-hour drive back to the city was a forbidding prospect. But he couldn't bring himself to ask for the use of Keeper's guest room.

'Listen, Jack. I'm sorry if I upset you. But you do see this is different, not like other times. Getting bounced out of school, busted for selling marijuana, that's child's play compared with this.'

'Sure. I see.' Keeper turned to Fall. 'The kid has graduated. From a little shitheap to a big one. Well, why should I get involved? I don't know him. God, you remember the fight for those precious visiting rights? And what did that add up to? Busting my hump for a chance to take this kid to a circus, buy him a turtle, ask a few questions about his dog. He got older and I asked about his girls instead of his pets. I must have bored him to death. So I faced it. He was hers, all hers.'

There was a silence.

Fall went to the front door and pulled it open. He paused.

'That window I broke, there's glass all over the kitchen. Want me to clean it up?'

'No,' Keeper muttered.

Fall pulled the door of the house shut behind him. He got into the back of his car and cramped himself, lying down, onto the seat. Eventually he went to sleep.

Evidence

Near the cracked mirror above the sink was an electric outlet with a toggle switch beside the plugholes and the figures 110–220 v. stamped into its plastic safety plate. An arrow pencilled onto the stained yellowish wall pointed to the fixture, its tail underlining two scrawled words: RAZZER ONLY. In his many restless trips to the mirror, Roy Keeper had found the proviso repeatedly comforting; it was, at the moment, the best clue to his future.

He had been brought to the building through narrow streets and back alleys, hustled through a door that led up a flight of wooden stairs to a dingy uncarpeted corridor lined on both sides with closed, numbered doors. Through one of these they had shoved him roughly, into a room furnished with a sway-backed bed, one chubby sweat-mottled easy chair, a chest of drawers, and a wooden table with rickety legs. The largest area of remaining floor space was covered by a round grey rug that looked like a compressed pancake of pure dust. Yet Roy did not feel direly oppressed. The large unbarred window was open a crack, admitting an ample flow of brisk refreshing sea air. And the door, though it had been locked from the outside, was held solely by an ordinary hotel-type mechanism. If this were a prison, he decided, it must be reserved for those enemies of the state whose political style might return to fashion at any moment. Or trespassing tourists earmarked for a good scare.

Most likely it was not a prison at all. The razor outlet implied the room's use by travellers who brought along such bourgeois conveniences as electric razors. This might even be the hotel where Intourist steered visiting Americans with their steam irons and coffeepots. If any American ever visited Batumi.

So it seemed they had believed him. Perhaps the questions

they had asked after taking him aboard the patrol boat were routine.

Do you work for the CIA?

What is your connection with the CIA?

How long have you been an agent for the CIA?

Endlessly repeated, the initials became meaningless. Or so he could think now. In the comparative comfort of the hotel room Roy could afford to consider the ludicrous side of what had actually been a terrifying few minutes.

The markings on the patrol boat had been barely distinguishable when the first shell had whistled across his bow, drenching him in the spray from its explosive plunge. At first he had assumed they could not see he was stalled, drifting, and were firing to prevent his escape. But when the sea had drunk in a fourth and fifth screaming salvo, he had known they simply intended to sink him. There was no other reason to keep up the barrage. They had been close enough after the third shot to see he was heaved-to. Roy could be certain of that; the distance between the boats had shrunk sufficiently for him to discern a smile on the face of the cannoneer.

The sixth shell had changed his mind again. Fired from such a short range that Roy could see a gap in the gunner's front teeth. At this distance, if the Russians were still sending in near-misses, it was not an accident. Then, what was the intention? Perhaps they had taken him for a stray Turkish fisherman from down the coast, would chase him away after a harassment which, when reported to others, would discourage further carelessness.

Capitalizing on such a mistake, however, had not tempted Roy. He had been cautioned more than once during his briefing to react to any hostile situation in a manner always consistent with his cover story. What would that be in this hostile situation? he wondered. What would a carefree tourist out for a joyride on the Black Sea be doing while half a dozen monster shells sizzled the immediate vicinity?

The first thing he decided was to admit his origin, shout at them in English. And say what? Did it matter? He would hardly be heard above the patrol boat's diesels.

'Pigs!' he shrieked. 'I'm unarmed!'

SPEAK WHEN SPOKEN TO. No interpreter was needed to translate the burst from the Russian machine gun. The patrol boat circled three times at close range, the wake from its wheeling high-speed turns chopping across itself, kicking Roy's craft into a bucking frenzy. And all the while the machine gun spit bullets in an endless stream, perforating the rotting hull. Deck and engine house burbled with hundreds of small springs, water and kerosene from the fuel tank running over each other in miniature cataracts.

Oddly, the effect of the attack on Roy's psychological defences diminished as it went on. In all the shelling and gunfire, his only injury was a nick on the back of one hand caused by a flying wood chip. The extravaganza of noise and destruction had obviously been meant solely to intimidate him. When the shelling stopped, he suspected, the worst would be over. It would take a higher authority than a patrol's captain to order the kind of treatment that would later have to be justified by bringing serious charges, accusations that would have to be proven. And what proof did they have, since he had been caught, luckily, before the contact was made?

By the time Roy had been taken aboard the patrol boat, the deck he left behind was already more than half under water, sinking fast. It seemed only one more extraneous show of force to be held at the rail by a burly scowling sailor and made to watch as another series of shells reduced the fishing boat to a pitiful island of flotsam.

The Russian captain had scoffed at the passport Roy presented, and questioned him rudely. But Roy remained inwardly calm, feigning his increasingly submissive responses to be 'consistent with his cover story'. He was in trouble, he knew, but it was certain to be cleared up. The lies he had told were unspectacular, they would be swallowed. They might stick for a day or two in official throats, but they would be swallowed.

As the boat knifed towards Batumi, Roy was confident that it was only the first leg of a journey back to where he had come from.

The hotel room buoyed his confidence. For all its faults, it must be one of the best in the house. The window commanded a sweeping view of the harbour. Off to one side Roy could see huge structures encased in mazes of pipeline, topped by soaring cylinders that trailed black smoke into the sky from their mouths. Refineries. Closer by were the docks from which the scent of citrus awaiting shipment drifted on the breeze – a heady odour dominated by one particular fragrance that Roy found familiar but irritatingly unnameable. Directly opposite the window, running past the hotel front, was a concrete promenade lined with palm trees. It looked like a pleasant place to stroll, though it was empty now.

It was dawn; a sullen tropical rain was falling. Roy looked at his watch. Six o'clock. He had spent ten hours pacing from the window to the mirror and back, waiting for some sign that the machinery of release was beginning to clank forward. There had been one visitor, a chunky young blonde girl. An hour after his arrival she had brought a bowl of thick tasteless soup. No one else had come since. Yet he remained less worried than bored. In view of the time he had been arrested, it was not alarming that they had left him alone. He had landed in Batumi at eight o'clock the previous evening. The local bureaucrats who would deal with his case were home by then or dining out, maybe dancing at the pavilion somewhere along the promenade from which a mélange of Slavic folk music and Dixieland had been audible until midnight. If they had neglected him, it was one more bit of evidence that his infraction was being taken lightly. They hadn't hurried to question him, left their dinners half-eaten, the dance unfinished. They had left the problem for morning, for regular office hours.

He lay down on the bed, analysed his predicament again and reassured himself. And then, exhausted, his assurances spent, he wondered if his confidence came only from inexperience, ignorance. What a ridiculous hybrid he was, thought Roy, a crossbreeding of amateur spy and dilettante idealist.

At that moment, just on the edge of sleep, he realized what was sending out that lovely aroma from the docks. Tangerines.

He rose into consciousness riding the smell of smoke. Opening his eyes, Roy saw a man sitting beside the bed, thin legs crossed, a pipe viced tightly between his teeth. An aura of professorial detachment surrounded the man. Heavy gold-framed spectacles straddled a thin sharp nose, bushy eyebrows creeping over the tops like rampant vines over a garden wall. His hair, dark blond and well cut, surprised Roy as did the clothes, a well-fitted tweed jacket over charcoal flannel slacks. Everything about him contradicted the standard Russian image for interrogator. Where was the squat bully with greasy pompadoured black hair, wearing a drab baggy suit?

The man took the pipe from his mouth. 'So. We wake. Very obliging.'

Obliging? Had they injected him while he slept, given a drug that would jolt him awake helplessly spilling out the truth? Roy pulled himself up on his elbows and checked the sleeves of his denim shirt; both were half rolled as he'd left them. He felt no aches in either arm.

'I have only a moment ago let myself in,' said the man. 'I ask you quietly to wake, you obey. An excellent beginning. If your conscious self will co-operate as easily as the unconscious, we will have a successful meeting.' His accent was extremely slight. 'Please excuse me for being so long to come, Mr Keeper. But I could not see you without first doing my homework.'

'Who are you?' Roy said cautiously.

'I am the official greeter to all delegates from CIA who visit our little corner of Russia. By name Gavril Schub; by profession, local officer of the Soviet Committee for Security – if you prefer, the KGB. How do you do.' He smiled and held out his hand.

It was prudent to accept the courtesy, Roy thought, despite the context in which it was offered. He sat up, swung his legs to the floor and gave Schub's outstretched hand one brisk pump. 'Look. I have nothing to do with the CIA. Nothing. I explained that to your patrol captain about half a million times. I got lost, that's all. I'm just a poor sonofabitch tourist who lost his way.'

Schub swivelled his head to examine the room. 'You are satisfied with your accommodations?'

Roy felt strangely embarrassed, much as if Schub had changed the subject to avoid some painful secret of his life – an insane wife, an idiot child.

'They're not bad,' Roy said.

Schub's bushy eyebrows lifted and swelled, two small furry animals inhaling. 'Not bad? This is a hotel, my boy. You could be in prison. Under the circumstances our hospitality should not be taken lightly.'

'What do you expect me to say – I'm crazy about the room? There's only one thing you really have to know: if I've done anything to hurt your mother country.' Roy looked hard into the dark eyes behind the glinting lenses. 'I haven't.'

'Yes,' Schub assented, 'that is quite true. Because you were prevented.' From his jacket pocket he took a penknife and pried open one blade. With great attention to the task, he began scraping the bowl of his pipe. 'There are rats in the prison. It is always a problem; the prison is very near the waterfront. We do what we can, but the creatures breed so quickly, especially in seaports. Usually no more than a month after complete fumigation, reports come again from the cell blocks. In one, a man wakes in the night to find half a toe nibbled away. In another, some poor soul has lost the tip of his nose. Day by day the complaints grow until almost every cell has its victim. The guards joke that it is better to feed the rats on prisoners than have our export foods destroyed on the docks.' He emptied the charred scrapings from his pipe onto the floor. 'But we are not inhumane. We have our exterminations once a year. It is your good fortune, Mr Keeper, that this year's is scheduled to begin in a day or two. When our patrol radioed news of your arrest, it was thought that to put you in our prison at the very height of the rat season, so to speak, would be poor manners indeed. A kindness, you agree? A favour, I frankly admit, I would like you to return.'

'How?' Roy barked. 'By telling you what you want to hear? Jesus, you people are obsessed with the CIA.'

Schub shrugged. 'Aren't we all?' he said drily.

'Listen, that homework of yours' – Roy worked to suppress a tremble he heard in his own voice – 'I suppose it included a chat with the captain of the patrol. I told him everything. Just check it out. You'll find my clothes in Room Six of a small hotel in Konila, a Turkish fishing village down the coast. I forget the name of the hotel, but it's the only one in town. And there's a fisherman named Goju who rented me his boat for the day. I wanted to see the coast from the water, find a deserted place for a swim. I wasn't spying.'

Schub uncrossed his legs and leaned forward. 'I do not doubt we will find your clothes in Room Six of the hotel in Konila - called, by the way, "The Alexandria". And no doubt some roughneck will turn up to say he rented you a boat. Who should know better than I that missions like yours are not lightly undertaken? Tracks are laid, alibis arranged. All well and good, unless one is caught in the act. That is the case here, is it not?'

'What are you talking about? Caught in what act?'

Schub sat back. 'We have evidence.'

Now Roy could not fight off the terror, a lightning disease crawling through his limbs. He said nothing. He had begun to recognize that Schub was not here to ask questions, but to parade his knowledge.

The Russian had taken out a leather pouch and was fastidiously repacking his pipe with tobacco. 'We have picked up the student you were coming to meet,' he said, 'in the Gardens.'

'Gardens?' Roy murmured. 'What Gardens?'

Schub ignored the question. 'It's a shame you weren't caught with him. At least then you would have seen them. They are lovely. Do you know we have there fifteen thousand different varieties of flora?'

Roy stared at the Russian. The praise of flowers juxtaposed with threatening accusations struck him as insane, chatter from a mad tea party.

'Come now, Mr Keeper,' Schub went on. 'Don't pretend you know nothing of Batumi's Botanical Gardens. It's our main tourist attraction. A lovely place to meet,' he added with malicious irony.

Roy was speechless, incredulous. This had nothing to do with him! His contact was to be made on water, miles from land. Unless . . . there had been some mistake, the instructions fouled. Could things have been that carelessly planned? Or was it a mundane bureaucratic screw-up, one of the triplicate forms lost on a trip between pigeonholes? No! It couldn't happen that way. But the alternative was no more likely: By some freak coincidence his arrest had occurred simultaneously with the discovery of an unrelated plot; two undergrounds had collided, collapsing their separate tunnels.

'He was in our hands an hour before you were apprehended,' Schub said. 'Your mission would have failed even if you had landed, instead of being taken at sea.'

'This is all mixed up,' Roy said desperately. 'I was never going to – I wasn't meeting anyone, anywhere.'

'Please. It is useless to deny.' Schub lilted the words, the inflection of a forebearing schoolmaster awaiting a child's confession to a prank. 'Up to the moment of your arrest, your accomplice was quite unwary. He greeted our agent in English. That is the language you speak ...'

'Along with a few hundred million other people. Is that what you call evidence?'

'You do not accept the definition? Fair enough. Then you must understand that I cannot accept your circumstantial alibis as a defence. It does not matter where we can find your suitcases, but where you are found. It does not matter what boat you say you rented, but what boat you arrive in.' From the pocket bulging with smoker's accessories, Schub withdrew a matchbox. He shook it to make sure there were matches inside; a few sticks clacked against the wooden walls. The sound, Roy thought, was very similar to the warning rattle of a Wyoming diamondback about to strike. 'We have the raft, Mr Keeper, and that is worth a thousand words.'

'You have what ...?'

Schub struck a match and held it to his pipe. He spent a long time sucking at the flame, more time than he needed. 'A rubber raft,' he said finally. 'The markings have naturally been removed, but there are clues to the place of manufacture. It will easily be recognized as the sort of craft which would be used to put you clandestinely ashore from a larger vessel – from, let us say, a submarine of the United States Navy.'

Roy bolted to his feet. 'That won't work. You bastards, you'll never make that work.' He paced the room in a frenetic pattern. 'Evidence! Evidence, for Chrissake. And then you come up with that. Well, listen: I have my story, I have that one story and I'm sticking to it. I'll tell it every chance I get. You pin your lies on me and somehow it'll come out.'

Schub nodded, puffing his pipe. A halo of smoke broke up and avalanched lazily off his hair. 'It will indeed come out, just as you say. Your side and ours. At your trial.'

Roy stared dumbly at the Russian, who kept nodding, the steady silent yes yes yes daring Roy to disbelieve. But he did. The bluff was too audacious. They really were treating him like a tourist, thinking he'd fall apart so easily. 'You'd better hold that trial in some dark cellar, then. Because the lies won't make it any other way.'

The nod continued, patronizing now, the schoolmaster again. 'We have all we need, Mr Keeper. But for one thing. That brings me to the favour I came to ask.' He pulled a folded piece of white paper from an inside pocket of his jacket. 'This is a confession I would like you to sign. As a token of appreciation for the gesture on our side. You remember: the rats?' He tossed the paper on the bed and stood up. 'You may think I am asking more than has been given in return. You may, because you have never had one of those yellow squealing pests chew away your foot. Neither have I. So I will understand if you must think very carefully before signing this.' He crossed the room to where Roy was standing. 'Hundreds of reasons not to sign will come to you. Believe me, please: It will be for your good to ignore them and do what I ask. You will not believe me, though, will you? I am the big bad Russian.' He clapped his hand rather sympathetically on Roy's shoulder and went to the door.

As Schub opened the door, Roy remembered to ask: 'I want to see someone from the American Embassy. Now. Today. You tell them I'm here!'

Schub walked out. The door remained wide open until a uniformed soldier leaned into view, grabbed the knob, and pulled it shut.

The glimpse of the guard was a fresh shock. Roy tried to minimize it, to dismiss it as an effect staged to intimidate him further. If they were pressing him this hard to incriminate himself there couldn't be any real evidence. The arrested student must be as conveniently invented as the raft. Submarine! Comic-book stuff. He was safe as long as nothing was signed, certified. They couldn't know what he had really come for.

But a moment later, when he went to the bed and read the paper, the wall Roy had built against fear cracked and tumbled. They did know what he had come for. Exactly.

Wet Paint

Fall's reception room was filled with reporters, sprawling on the formal leather chairs, chatting in groups against the walls. As Keeper entered, the loose assemblage coagulated around him. A camera eye advanced, a blinding light fixed over it.

'Will you be going to Russia, Mr Keeper?' asked a voice behind the light.

'Get that away,' Keeper snarled.

Fall came pushing through the reporters, grabbed Keeper and took him back into his office, a large sunny cage of bookshelves. The door shut slowly against the thrusting mass of newsmen.

'I was invaded this morning,' Keeper fumed as soon as they were alone. 'Some reporters climbed the fence around my house. I'd sue the bastards, except there's one hitch. These intruders say they broke in at the request of my lawyer.'

'I didn't tell them to break in,' Fall blurted defensively. 'I knew they were going out to your house. To save me the trip, I asked them to tell you about this letter.' He waved towards his desk where a piece of paper lay on the bright-green blotter. 'I suppose it was all the excuse they needed. But it's your fault, too, Jack – closing yourself off. If I could have reached you by phone –'

'I didn't turn it off.'

'Well, nobody could get through. The operator said –'

'I know. I called my number from your downstairs lobby: "Not in service." It wasn't my idea.'

'Oh. Phone company goofed, I guess.' Fall motioned Keeper to a chair.

But Keeper continued pacing nervously, pantherish. 'Sure, they made a mistake. Or maybe the gremlins heard me say I wanted to be left out.'

'Doesn't look as if you do, Jack, walking around dressed that way. The old hermit. You're too good a story; they'll never let you alone.'

Under Fall's gaze, Keeper became aware of the clothes he had thrown on to leave his house, a frayed pair of blue jeans and an old sweatshirt.

'Let's see this letter,' he said, snatching up the paper as he dropped into a chair beside Fall's desk.

It was a piece of stationery from a hotel in the city. At the top was a small escutcheon, the mongrel heraldry of commerce. Wine glasses, prancing tigers, knives and forks and a fleur de lis were distributed in the crest's quadrants. Ornate printing said: 'The Barony – a Noble Concept in Hostelry'.

The handwriting underneath was small and shapely, the product of penmanship drills in a one-room Wyoming schoolhouse. It reminded him of what he had loved in her, the odd mix of daintiness with a coltish tomboy quality nurtured in her outdoor upbringing. He was thinking of happier days as he began to read:

Dear Jack,

I couldn't get to you by phone, so I'm writing. For whatever it's worth, you are his father and entitled to know that everything is being well taken care of. Our government people are doing all they can. Arrangements have been made for me to go to Russia and attend the trial. I'm sure you'll be relieved to know that neither Roy nor I will mind that you keep your time, money, and good wishes for yourself.

Susan

He lingered over the last line, weighing its bitter tone. At long last it seemed she had ceased to love him, to forgive. Long after the divorce and his remarriage, she had always been kind in her letters. With Roy in the biggest trouble of his life, she had finally climbed on the bandwagon that would lay the blame at his door.

More irksome than the words, however, was the paper itself. He had not been handed the original letter, but an office photocopy.

'What's the idea of this?' Keeper asked sharply. 'Where's the original?'

'They took it.' Fall was sitting behind his desk.

'Who?'

'The men who brought it, two of them. It was also their idea to get word to you through the reporters. They said it was urgent.'

'A letter telling me to mind my own damn business?'

'I didn't know what the letter said when they first walked in. I just did what they told me. They sat around for a while as if they planned to wait for you, then they gave up and left. That's when they copied the letter. For government files, they said.'

Keeper examined the paper in his hand. Under what subheading in what file would it gather dust? In the history of one decayed love it might be significant. But what else could possibly give it importance?

'There's a law against it, isn't there?' he said.

'What?'

'Tampering with mail.'

'That isn't mail, Jack. Technically it's a government dispatch. That's what they told me, anyway, and I didn't think it was worth running to the law library to check. You can read what she says. That's what counts.'

Keeper walked to the window. By a corner news-stand twelve storys below, a cluster of people were buying newspapers. Roy's story had graduated to the headlines. Despite a struggle with the October wind to keep their papers from being blown apart, the people were avidly reading the newspapers as soon as they bought them.

'Funny how it works,' said Keeper. 'I wanted to stay out of this. And I get signals saying "Fine . . . stay out . . . get lost." Only somehow that makes it harder. Like WET PAINT signs. You can pass one and not give it a thought. But when they're tacked up in a row, one after another, it's like a dare. You've got to stick your finger in it.'

'I don't understand, Jack.'

Keeper held up the photocopy. 'That's what I read here, "wet paint".' He crumpled the paper into a ball and crammed it in his pocket.

'You said a row . . .'

'The phone, that's another. And my car wouldn't start, dead

battery. I was cut off completely. Then there was one more; it showed on the way to town. I needed a lift, so I rode in with a few reporters. They also told me the latest news, about the trial, the evidence. It was pretty hard to sit through with a straight face. Because I thought I knew something they didn't, something I've greased a lot of palms to keep hidden. That Roy has the kind of record that would blacklist him from any government work, much less anything top secret.' He came to the desk and leaned across. 'But guess what, Andy? They told me that, too. The papers know it all: the drug busts, draft dodging — every bit of it.'

Fall responded slowly. 'That's good, isn't it? I mean, to save Roy maybe it had to come out. I suppose Susan told them.'

'Maybe she did, thinking it would do some good. But that isn't how these reporters got the information. They just did their job, made routine checks when the story broke: school records, draft boards, police. It was all there once they dug deep enough. We assumed it was still buried because the story hasn't shown up in print. But they had it.' Keeper's face hardened. 'They just aren't going to use it.'

'Why not?'

'Because somebody asked them not to.'

'Who?'

'The reporters couldn't tell me. It doesn't happen at their level. But there aren't many places a request like that can come from and get results.'

Fall pursed his lips and whistled. 'I knew it was big ... those two guys delivering that letter ... I had a feeling.' He rotated his swivel chair to look at the leather sofa at the end of his office, recalled the grim presences of the two men who had sat there. 'They never smiled, hardly talked except to tell me what they wanted and how to get it done. Orders, Jack, they gave orders. When they said urgent, you had to believe it. The way they handled that letter, it was like "top secret" was stamped all over it.'

'And then they left a copy for everyone to see,' Keeper observed sourly. 'It stinks, Andy. There's something wrong with this from the top down. Roy couldn't be spying; they'd never enlist a kid like that.'

Fall chewed on his lip. Then he said, 'There are certain things Roy might've been used for.'

'What?' Keeper snapped.

'Remember, in our war, how the Japs used kamikazes. I mean, sometimes you have to get the most reckless kind of person. For an assassination, say . . .'

'You think Roy would have gone on a suicide mission?' Keeper almost laughed. 'Not in a million years. Roy isn't a fanatic, a superpatriot, or a nut with a homicidal streak. He likes his good times. That's the only thing that's ever landed him in trouble.'

'But if he's going on trial, Jack, there must be some evidence.'

'If there isn't, the Russians will make it up.' Keeper paused. 'What beats me is that the best available proof is all in Roy's favour. Who'd believe that he'd dodge the draft and then go to work as a spy? If his background came out, the Russians would have a much harder time framing him. But our side is holding back.'

'How do you explain it?' Fall said.

'I can't. So I'll swallow my pride, use my money instead of my brains.' Keeper moved towards the door. 'Call the men in homburgs, Andy, the bosses for those two lumps who were here before. Tell them I want the answers.'

Fall made a flustered rush to stop Keeper from leaving. 'Jack, you can't expect answers if there's some secret thing –'

'Get them,' Keeper insisted. 'Or I'll make all the trouble money can buy.'

'I'll do what I can,' Fall promised quickly. 'Where can you be reached?'

'I'm going to have a talk with Susan.'

'But Jack, she flew out this morning.'

'Where to?'

'Russia.'

Keeper paused. 'Did you talk to her?'

Fall shook his head. 'She was in Washington under wraps. She stopped over in New York before taking the plane, but by the time this letter came and I knew the hotel, she'd gone.'

Keeper nodded slowly. 'I want those answers,' he said softly to Fall and opened the door.

'So where can I reach you?'

'I don't know yet,' Keeper said over his shoulder. 'Find me.'

As he came out of the office, a warm beer-scented wind of words came at him. This time Keeper stood placidly, let the reporters pack themselves around him. His eyes went from one to the other, looking straight at them. He knew now that their pursuit of him wasn't a search for news, but for self-justification. They needed proof that their concealments were right, necessary.

As he searched their faces disdainfully, voices became quieter, questions were choked back half-finished. Suddenly they were all silent. And when Keeper moved forward without speaking, the thick mob of men parted before him.

Medal

The tears trickling in two lines from the inside corners of the man's eyes were not the clear fluid of cleansing sorrow, but ugly purplish marks on the skin. When Roy had first noticed the man across the walled yard, he had thought the tears were real, darkened by some diseased excretion. In the prison it would be easy enough to develop such a hideous abscess. A hand used to pick up something from the floor, later to rub one's eyes, stinging tired from the perpetually burning electric bulbs. Infection, even blindness. At least half the prisoners lined along the walls had a dirty bandage wrapped around some part of their bodies, a finger, an ear. Infections were amply fed by the filth everywhere. Even the treatment, the 'bandages', spread disease. The prisoners had to make their own from the only dispensable source, their dirty clothes. Why wouldn't a man cry in nightmare colours?

But as Roy looked at the tears now he realized that they did not move, did not well and flow down. They were tattoos, an epitaph in blood and scar for a part of his humanity that had died, the ability to weep.

In another place, on other days, the sight would have horrified Roy. But here he understood. How long would it be before he made some such desperate gesture against himself? Wasn't he the one to punish, to blame for being here? This is what the prisoners must come to believe. They were faced with an immutable system, insensitive to their hatred; easier than hating the system, less wasteful of their passion, was to hate one's self for being its victim. And demonstrate the hatred in self-mutilation.

Similarly, Roy felt less betrayed by the faceless link who had dutifully reported to the Russians than by himself. As a search for pleasure life had run smoothly. It was in the diamond field

of ideals that he had stumbled. Not political ideals, but roman-
tic dreams. He had done it for her. The fantasies of adventure,
of 'helping to build a better world', he saw now how foolish
they were. He had done it because she believed in it – or because it would make her believe in him. Remembering her,
knowing he would do it again for the same reasons, he could
not blame his betrayal on anyone but himself.

The tattooed tears were getting clearer, closer. The man must
be moving, changing places one by one with the prisoners next
to him in line. The movement had been so careful that Roy
had not seen it occur. Now he forced memories out of his mind,
clamped the present into place. He wanted to catch the next
move. He had the impression somehow that the man with
tattooed tears was manoeuvring to speak to him.

For a long time the man didn't move, didn't look anywhere
but straight ahead.

Roy lifted his arm, jerked his wrist free of the shirt cuff, then
remembered they had taken his watch. His watch and the laces
of his sneakers. He looked at his wrist anyway, verifying the
memory. The watch was gone. Roy turned back to the man
with the tattooed tears.

Had he moved again? Roy couldn't be sure. The prisoners
looked so much alike. So many had beards; they weren't allowed
to shave themselves. Nor were they distinguished by their clothing. They did not wear uniforms, but their own shirts, pants,
and jackets. All were soiled beyond distinction except for the
numerous rips that showed in slightly different places. Tattooed
Tears stood out plainly enough, but it was hard to tell if he had
advanced past another prisoner. Roy studied the details: If the
man changed places again, he would be switching with a prisoner who had a bandage tied around his knee, outside the
trousers.

But it would be another long wait. A guard was passing along
that section of the yard, leaning close over the men to make
certain their backs were pressed up against the cold stone wall.

They had been marched into the rectangle of hard ground at
dawn, given a breakfast of rough grain and water mixed in a
bowl to drink where they stood. They were to remain there,

lined up, until the fumigation was completed. Schub had not lied. This was the annual rat extermination, and Roy had been held apart from it in the hope of getting the confession gratefully signed.

When Schub had returned to the hotel room and found the torn bits of paper on the bed, he had attempted no further persuasion. 'It would have been easier,' he had said, scraping his pipe thoughtfully. Then he had left, again without replying to Roy's demand to see someone from the Embassy.

There had been one more effort to break him down at the hotel. The blonde girl who served his food had appeared again. This time, while setting out a plate of fish and vegetables, she had begun to cry. Then, in her garbled English, she had reported overhearing some talk of sending Roy to prison. Maybe it had been true. Perhaps she had been a frightened girl in need of solace, or a compassionate peasant comforting another lost soul. But he had steeled himself against responding when she moved into his arms. Too quickly, he thought, much too quickly. It was equally possible that she was KGB, their casting for the irresistible feminine ideal, chubby and sweet-faced. He had held her for a few moments, making no move to test the limits of her compassion. She had asked if he planned to sign the confession; he answered no. She had cried a little more before going. Listening at the door, Roy had heard her sobbing continue, fading away down the outside corridor.

That afternoon they had taken him out through the back door of the mysterious hotel and put him in a car. After a short drive, it had stopped at the front gate of the prison. It was a low, warehouse-type of building, four two-storey wings boxing in an exercise yard, situated somewhere in the industrial district.

Moving him to the prison had not been a surrender in their battle to obtain a confession. A typed copy had been lying on the burlap pillow of his cell bunk when they locked him in. He had torn it in half, using the paper to cover some excrement stinking in the corners. Later a passing guard had slipped another copy through the cell door. Roy had covered some more filth. The copies kept coming. A typed original followed by a series of seven carbons, getting progressively fuzzier and less readable. Then a new original would appear, sharp and clear, a reminder that hunger for retribution did not fade with the copies.

Roy started saving the confessions, welcoming the smooth paper to coat the itchy burlap of the thin mattress and pillow. Even then, though the guards could see he was no longer destroying them, the duplicates kept coming. They would pile up, Roy imagined, until he signed one.

I, ROY KEEPER, A CITIZEN OF THE UNITED STATES OF AMERICA, ADMIT THAT I HAVE COLLABORATED OF MY OWN DESIRE IN ACTIVITIES CONTRARY TO INTERNATIONAL CODES OF LAW AND GOOD WILL, AND EXPRESSLY FOR-BIDDEN BY THE UNION OF SOVIET SOCIALIST REPUBLICS. IN SPECIFIC, I HAVE CONSPIRED TO RECEIVE FROM THE HANDS OF CORRUPT AND CRIMINAL INTELLECTUAL ELE-MENTS THE LITERARY MANUSCRIPT ENTITLED 'THE MUSH-ROOM CAVE' BY SEMYON LYNDUSHKIN, DISCREDITED MEMBER OF THE WRITERS UNION NOW DECEASED. THIS MEMOIR, THOUGH KNOWN TO BE A FALSE DOCUMENTATION OF SLANDERS AGAINST THE SOVIET UNION, WAS TO BE PUBLISHED ILLEGALLY TO DEFAME THE SOVIET UNION AMONG ALL PEOPLES OF THE WORLD.

TO SIGN HEREON

Though the facts were contorted by the heavy load of pro-paganda they were made to carry, they were essentially accur-ate. Even Schub's threatened lies – the raft, the student Roy was supposed to have met on land – had not been mentioned. As it stood, the confession was a barbed reminder of how easy the job had sounded when it had been proposed. Easy! For them. There must have been a plant among his recruiters. The first original and seven copies might have been typed and waiting long before he arrived.

Or was he literally his own betrayer? There was nothing stated on the paper that hadn't been part of her proposition. Maybe in some Left Bank café, or at some student party, he had scoffed aloud at the absurdity of his being enlisted. He had seen a slogan once in a book of World War II news pictures: 'Loose lips sink ships.' He could have been careless. Even the letter to his mother had been unwise, he saw now. But nobody had warned him. He had seen too much hokey espionage on television and in movies to take it seriously. Easy. It had sounded so easy ...

A wheelbarrow went by loaded with dead rats, a grotesque fringe of tails dangling over the side. The barrows had been going by all day, emerging from different doors of the prison, traversing the yard to disappear through the main gate. This time as the gate was opened and the barrow went out, a prisoner called out a Russian phrase. The voice was gruff and bitter, but whatever was said made the other prisoners laugh. What joke could have raised laughter in this hell, Roy wondered. A shout to the rats, perhaps: 'Good-bye, pals, we envy you your freedom.' He shuddered at the possibility that someday such humour might amuse him, too. He might be hopeless enough to join the rueful laughter.

The other prisoners would not stop. Restless from a day of standing under constant guard, they extruded the initial reflex into a ritual, jostling one another repeatedly, their laughter getting louder, more hysterical. The guards tried to quiet them and find the disruptive joker, but exterminating powder sifting down from the prison windows had formed a cloud over the yard. Though it was faint, forms and faces still showing through, the silvery haze gave an illusion of immunity to the prisoners. More began to shout, turning their laughs into rude brays, cackles, hoots. The four guards grew correspondingly more flustered, ran back and forth erratically as though pursuing a chicken for beheading. The prisoners grew more excited. On either side of him, Roy heard the men begin chanting two syllables: 'Krisa! Krisa! Krisa!'

Suddenly one of the guards raced across the yard and drove his rifle butt into the side of one prisoner's head. The long dash had looked like a matador's run before sinking the sword, the blow struck on the run.

The yard was silent. The men stood flat against the wall, one break in the line where a crumpled figure lay on the ground. When the wheelbarrow returned through the gate, now empty of rats, the guard barked an order at the prisoner pushing it. The prisoner stopped the barrow beside the victim, loaded him into it, and carted him inside the prison. A dark splotch of blood-soaked earth marked the place where the prisoner's head had lain, cracked by the rifle butt. The guard walked over and shifted some dry unstained dust over the spot with his foot. The moment of resistance was over, eradicated.

Roy felt a coiling thing writhe in his stomach, trying to unwind. Desperation, greater than before. He had tasted the instant of freedom, throwback to the real world. He had wanted to call out, to protest; for a moment, without understanding the chant, he had joined in. But here the consequences crashed down. Skulls were split, and silence returned.

Sign! Get out!

But if he signed, they would never let him out. He would spend his youth here, or someplace like it.

The tattooed tears. In the commotion, Roy had forgotten. He had sensed the man was coming to talk with him. Maybe he would offer a chance of escape, a deal in return for the confession. He might be co-operating with the KGB to earn his own reprieve. It was a fragile hope, but Roy propped it up, an egg on a knife edge.

He glanced towards the man.

Nine places! He had taken advantage of the disruption to move nine places past the man with the bandaged knee. But there were still many men separating them. Seventeen, Roy counted. And a corner to be turned. Switching slowly to avoid attracting the guard's attention, it might take another hour, even two. Would the rats hold out long enough for them to meet and talk?

A sick smile came to Roy's lips. Time measured in barrow loads of rats. God. It was happening already; he could see the gruesome jokes in this nightmare world.

An unintelligible whisper hushed in Roy's ear. Then he felt himself shoved hard with the hip of the man at one side, bumped through a slot as the man on the other stepped quickly away from the wall, then back in place after Roy had passed behind. They were all part of it! Helping to thrust him into the meeting with Tattooed Tears. The noisy disruption in the yard had been part of the plan. He was nudged again, a space opened for him to slip through. None of the prisoners looked at hi⸱

or at each other. Yet they functioned like a machine, synchronously shifting him along when no guard was looking.

As they switched the last place, moving together, Roy looked at the man. He had meant it to be quick, but his attention was held. The tears were drawn carefully, a horrific *trompe l'oeil* achieving a kind of beauty through perfectness of proportion, the tears of a saint in a Renaissance painting. The face, too, had a saintly air: thin, ascetic, grey hair cropped extremely short. It was a face the tears might have somehow glorified, if not for the eyes. Bleached rheumy eyes drawn wide into a permanent stare. The stare was more disturbing because it came out of no visible emotion. The eyes were not wide with terror or surprise or determination. They seemed to be made that way, without eyelids. But that wasn't it. There were lids.

The scar – that was the reason, Roy realized. It made a line across the forehead, nearly lost among many wrinkles. Evidently, it marked a place where a strip of skin had been excised, a wide strip; to close the gap the remaining skin had been stretched so tightly that the eyes were now held wide open.

'*Ossyol!* Don't look!' He spat out the angry words. And blinked; every muscle of his face was affected by the reflex, as though swallowing despite a very sore throat.

Roy snapped his head forward. A vision of the staring eyes stayed with him.

'You are him,' the man whispered, 'the American? Is truth?'

Roy didn't answer. The man's reproach had reminded him of the guards. They would certainly notice the change in this prisoner's position; those tears were instantly identifiable.

The man understood Roy's hesitation. ' 'Fraid you?'

'They can see,' Roy whispered.

A laugh rumbled low in the Russian's throat. 'See? They see nothing. They hear, yes, so we talk quiet.'

'They can see you've moved,' Roy insisted.

'How? Around they walk and around. For them it is all one wall.'

'But your face –'

'Faces they see less. We have not faces. We try, with the marks I try. But no. One time only I succeed. I had above my eyes saying there "we are the shit of Lenin". Ah!' Pride came through his whisper. 'Then I had face. They saw. But they cut and I am invisible again. Tears they don't see. Even these. Tomorrow, yesterday, are others like me; in the prisons many have done.'

Or maybe, thought Roy, they don't see because they've been directed not to.

'So talk is safe,' the Russian went on softly. 'Tell. Is truth?'

'What?'

'You come for writings of Lyndushkin?'

He must be co-operating with them. 'How do you know?'

The Russian sighed, the note sliding quickly back to the low pitch of secrecy. 'How do we know anything, *malchik*? We are in hell, it may be only the devil's gossip that we are alive. Today the gossip is you.' He lowered his voice even more. 'One of ours say he hear new man put in cell beside him. Then sees guard passing like hand of clock hour by hour, putting papers in new man's door. One time guard puts paper in wrong door. Is middle night, paper make small noise. Our man wakes thinking it is rat. He sees paper. To make no trouble if guard finds his wrong, man hammers words into mind, puts paper back in door. Morning, is gone. But this man moves to me by wall. I am only knows English. In ground he draw for me all the printing of his mind, one after one the letters. So I read.' He inclined minutely closer to Roy. 'Is truth?'

Roy judged the story. The guards had more than enough chances to make one simple error. But he gave up distrust reluctantly, preferring to think the prisoner would offer some deal for a confession. He faced the man again, wondering if he would object or allow the lapse, knowing the guards had instructions –

The eyes. Could their owner forgive this operation? Would he collaborate for any price with its authors? Wide and staring as they were, the eyes bulged yet more with anger and fear.

'Please! Turn away.' A begging tone.

Roy stared ahead at the yard.

The man went on, 'Understand, *malchik*, it is the way of safety here, always to look separate from each other, no matter how close. They not fear one man alone. About him they see nothing. It is two they fear, any two who seem together. About

41

these two they see everything. Two men together, that is the beginning of revolution.'

Roy's doubts collapsed. 'The paper is a confession,' he said. 'They want me to sign.'

'Yes. But is truth?'

Roy inclined his head, a camouflaged nod. Bending his neck he felt the stiffness of his joints, how much they all ached. He wanted to lie down.

'Why do you care?' he asked.

'This book mentioned. Is famous many years. There is long rumour Lyndushkin write three books. Two we know. For first they put him Siberia. Second he smuggle from there. The third, this they say are his memoirs. But is never found. Until now. Tell me about.'

'I can't. I didn't see them. They ...' The wish to explain flickered out. The man with tattooed tears offered no hope.

'Caught you,' said the Russian.

Roy said nothing. He felt the man looking at him, disregarding his own warning for an instant.

'You are tired to stand, eh? Not used?'

'Not used,' Roy admitted wearily.

A minute passed, then Tattooed Tears spoke again. 'Is great hero Lyndushkin. In special way. Because he was first one of them, the killers, torturers. Then he confessed his shame. He wrote it down and was made prisoner, and never stop his truth until they killed him.' The man's whispering voice revealed a throb. 'So for helping his spirit, you are hero, too. We think to give medal. What is medal here in this dunghole? Whatever they hate for us to have. This is medal and we give.'

Roy felt the man's hand groping at his side. He opened his own hand, touched the palm to the groping fingers, felt something put there. Cloth. No, cloth wrapped around something light and thin.

'Hold careful,' whispered Tattooed Tears. 'Must hide.'

Then he had gone, switching back one place with the man on his other side.

Very slowly, Roy looked down into the space between himself and the next prisoner. He opened his hand, palm towards the wall, and saw a piece of white cloth wrapping. With his thumb he worked away the folded ends.

He recognized the sensation, a cut so quick and clean that only the line of blood affirmed a wound. But he had to see the dull gleam of metal before he could believe that his medal, the precious citation for heroism, was nothing more than a rusty double-edged razor blade.

Briefing

'Madame is out,' the maid said starchily after Keeper had told her his name.

Keeper didn't recognize her; the servants had always quit after short periods of employment.

'I didn't come for a visit,' he said. 'I still have some clothes here. I want to change.'

The maid looked askance at his shabby outfit, then reluctantly stepped aside.

He crossed the foyer and went directly up the stairs. Woven into the carpet covering the twelve steps were the signs of the zodiac; the designs for her birth sign and his incorporated white asterisks. It embarrassed Keeper to confront these touches of décor, this one a reminder of his young second wife's belief in astrology. It seemed absurd now, all he had tolerated in the quest for rejuvenation – the fads, the modish tastelessness. Madeleine was twenty-three years younger. During the first two years of marriage she had let Keeper think he was satisfying her voracious sexual appetite. Then in the third year she had let him know there were others. At first he had cared, had tried to meet the challenge. This year, the fourth, he had given up.

Her bed was still unmade. Mechanically, he started going through the old bedroom routine, counting the cigarettes in the ashtrays as he always had after returning from a business trip. A few butts, no more than she would have smoked by herself. Of course, her latest might be a nonsmoker; there were more and more of them around.

He caught himself as he was scanning the dresser, looking for unfamiliar bottles of men's cologne. It didn't matter any more.

The clothes were still hanging where he had left them, in a

44

long closet behind mirrored doors. He chose a suit without deliberating and started to change.

He knew as soon as he had slipped one leg into the trousers. There was some extra material left flapping over his foot. Keeper was almost six feet tall; the owner of the suit would be a good two or three inches more. A big nonsmoker.

He kicked off the trousers and surveyed the other suits in the closet. He had always bought his clothes off-handedly and wasn't surprised that he recognized none of the fabrics. Perhaps only the one suit was not his own, perhaps none of them was his.

But his second selection fitted, and he found a shirt and tie he thought were his.

As he finished dressing, gave a final straightening tug to his tie, Keeper moved in front of the mirrored door. It had been more than a month, he realized now, since he had last taken a good look at himself, the kind of critical inspection he had put himself through daily when living with Madeleine. Searching for new wrinkles in his face, the deepening of old ones, assessing the depreciation of his body. He was amused to notice how long his hair had grown; it was getting shaggy.

Roy came into his mind. Oddly, not in any way connected to the mystery of his arrest. It was the last time they had seen each other that Keeper recalled. He had travelled to Wyoming. There were papers to be signed establishing a trust for Roy's education. While there, Keeper had taken Roy fishing one afternoon. Possibly because the activity demanded quiet, because Keeper hadn't felt constrained to make painfully inconsequential conversation, he had been less uncomfortable than usual with his fourteen-year-old son. For that afternoon, Keeper had even believed there was a bond between them that might last. But the distance had been too great. There had been no more meetings, just the reports on Roy's troubles, the telegrams from Susan asking for money to help. The only bonds between Keeper and Roy were bail bonds, and the extra payments that allowed the records of arrest to get lost at the back of the files.

Until today.

What had happened to Roy, what was he being used for?

With the distant afternoon fresh in his mind, the quiet

moments seated side by side on a riverbank, Keeper felt the bond again. However little they had seen each other, known about each other, they were father and son.

But what could he do to help? Staring back at his own eyes, Keeper saw the weakness still there. Could he accomplish anything alone? The machinery conspiring to convict Roy was not only immense, but invisible.

Keeper longed to have his confidence back, his daring; wanted it like some favourite possession that had been destroyed in a fire. For the first time he felt anguish at the loss. It was unrecoverable.

The anguish turned suddenly to rage. He was possessed by an urge to violence, to mar the beauty that had victimized him. If Madeleine had been in the bedroom now, Keeper thought, he would have given her a horrible beating. Might even have killed her.

The phone rang as Keeper descended the stairs. The maid appeared to answer the call in the foyer.

'Yes, he is,' Keeper heard her say. 'Just a –' She broke off and listened. Then with a peevish glance at the receiver, she replaced it in the cradle. 'That was for you, Mr Keeper. A man. He asked if you were here and I told him. He said to wait; he'll be here to see you in half an hour.'

'Who was he?'

'I don't know. He didn't say anything else, just hung up.'

Keeper went into the living room, a sanctum of chrome and glass guarded at the entrance by a plaster hotdog vendor. Pouring himself a drink, he thought about the anonymous call. It must be the result of his directions to Fall. Fast action. That meant, despite its size, the official machinery dealing with Roy's case was very sensitive. No time had been needed to burrow down to an elusive core. Fall had only to graze the outer skin and the heart had jumped.

Keeper anticipated meeting the nameless man, having the whole business explained; then he could let himself out of it. As he sat and waited, the maid brought Keeper a bundle of mail that had piled up in his absence. The bulk consisted of telegrams, their yellow envelopes standing out prominently. He opened these first. Most were from businessmen with whom he had once had profitable dealings, offers of sympathy and the use of any of their government connections. A few were from relatives, cousins of his or Susan's.

Then he came to a telegram which seemed to be part of a series.

REQUEST AGAIN CONTACT WYOMING STATE POLICE OVER-
TON BARRACKS

CAPT. RANDOLPH SEALING

Keeper started searching out the implied preceding message, but before it turned up the doorbell rang. He laid the mail aside and went out to the foyer.

'I'll keep it, thank you,' the visitor was saying. The maid had reached for his attaché case.

He was of medium height and build, with light-brown hair in a short collegiate cut, and pale-blue eyes. Keeper thought he looked less like a bureaucrat than the leader of a cub scout troop. The face was bland and boyish, a face from a Rockwell illustration. All-American. Yet, in spite of his dark conservative suit, the young man stood out as something special within the uniformed ranks of officialdom. Although he could be no more than thirty years old, he evinced none of the harried uncertainty of an underling. He exuded, rather, a sense of power. In the context of his boyish wholesomeness, however, the power he possessed seemed to be not so much a weapon as a toy. Power used playfully.

He spotted Keeper.

'Mr Keeper?'

'Right. Who are you?'

'I called . . .'

'Who are you?' Keeper repeated.

'Can we sit down first?' Without waiting for an answer, the visitor headed into the living room. Standing centre, he spent a few seconds deciding where to sit, then settled himself in a black leather chair that revolved on a chrome pedestal.

'Would you like to sit down?' the visitor said as he placed his case on the floor in front of his feet.

'I'll stand.' As Keeper moved deeper into the room, the visitor rotated his chair, holding Keeper in his direct gaze. He didn't speak until Keeper was still, leaning against a wall by the mantel.

'Mr Keeper, this must be made clear at the outset: We are responding to your lawyer's call not because of the irresponsible threats he transmitted on your behalf, but because it was the first indication we've had that you wish to be kept informed. The boy's mother had suggested you would prefer to remain uninvolved. Since you have asked for information, the Government is ready to oblige – on condition that the information is kept within a sphere of interested parties.'

'I don't care about satisfying anyone's curiosity but my own,' Keeper said. 'Now, for a start, let's see your credentials.'

The visitor accepted Keeper's harsh tone equanimously. Pulling a wallet from his inside jacket pocket, he rose and came across the room, smiling as though about to exhibit some prized baby pictures.

The card was behind a plastic window. At one side it showed a small full-faced photograph of the visitor, capturing every bit of his youthful sincerity. Facing this picture from the other edge of the card was an engraving, a schizoid eagle clutching an olive branch in one talon, and thirteen arrows in the other. In the space between the photograph and the national trademark a name appeared twice, once in print, once in signature: Stephen Parritt. There were no other marks, no organizational initials. Keeper slipped the card from behind its window and felt it between his fingers. It was laminated in plastic which bore the stamped impression of the government seal. He put the card back in its display pocket, then handed the wallet to Parritt.

'What does that prove?' he said.

'Put that card in a certain machine,' Parritt replied, 'and a green light will go on. That proves I'm who I say I am – not to you, but to the people I work for; they know that any other credentials could be forged.'

'Who do you work for?' Keeper asked.

'Sorry,' Parritt said, 'I can't disclose that. You'll have to judge me purely on what I say, whether I can tell you what you want to know. Now please sit down.'

Keeper regarded Parritt with a growing unease. The young man was like his identity card, encased in a smooth plastic coating. What was the lamination? The certainty that came of knowing secrets, perhaps, classified truths that decided the fate of unknowing millions. To some it might be a burden. But Parritt seemed to revel in the position, to flourish because of it. Keeper took Parritt's direction, content with the petty ploy of choosing a chair by the window; looking this way, Parritt would have the sun in his eyes.

'Would you mind moving to that chair?' Parritt pointed to a bulbous beanbag covered in blue vinyl. 'The sun is in my eyes.'

Keeper made the change.

'Thanks.' Parritt folded his hands in his lap. 'First and foremost, Mr Keeper, I can tell you your son is not working for us.'

'I never thought he was. But that's not the impression other people get when you censor his past record and refuse to deny this submarine story.'

Parritt painstakingly smoothed a wrinkle out of his pants. 'Your glib reference to the submarine story illustrates one of the problems we're up against. You see, the Russians rely on the bad habits of our press to jump to conclusions, blow things up, sensationalize. Are you aware the Russian news releases have very carefully avoided mentioning a submarine? All they've said is that your son was captured in a rubber raft –'

'Of U.S. Navy issue,' Keeper cut in sharply, 'which at the time of his capture was a good many miles offshore and damn far up the coast from the Turkish border. There are obvious implications to that story.'

'Maybe,' Parritt rejoined evenly. 'But we have pointed out that such rafts can be purchased easily in surplus stores and are popular for touring. Also that your son does have an outdoor background, having spent half his life in Wyoming.'

'I don't get it. You want people to believe Roy was on a camping trip? Then what's wrong with a flat denial? There was no submarine.'

Parritt kept an earnest silence for a moment. 'As I've said, all the Russians have done so far is plant a suspicion; they haven't spelled it out. If we issue denials of things that haven't actually been alleged, people would wonder why we're acting overanxious. That would only decide half the doubtful minds that it must be true.'

Keeper could accept that reasoning. Ever since the U-2 incident he had been inclined to accept official government denials as proof that the allegations being answered had at least a grain of truth. And how many incidents, formerly denied, had been proven true by the Pentagon Papers.

He switched the line of inquiry. 'Then why put the screws on our newspapers? Let them print what they know about Roy. That might be just as effective in blowing the Russian story.'

Parritt looked surprised. 'You want to see your son smeared?'

'I don't want to see him framed,' Keeper snapped. 'For what he's really done, yes, let him pay his dues.'

Quietly, Parritt said, 'He was trying to pay his dues, Keeper. Not through us, and not with anything we'd officially classify as espionage, but he was on a mission of sorts.' Parritt's lips twitched in an ephemeral smile. 'The kicker is, it wasn't even against the law, not strictly. That's why the Russians can't punish him unless they fake it, tack on other charges: illegal entry, anti-Soviet activities, espionage. They're going all out to nail him. Because the Commies believe that by stopping Roy, especially if they can make the espionage charge stick, they'll be eliminating a bigger threat to their power than all of our missiles.'

Keeper felt he was being fed clues like a contestant on a quiz show, the compère gloating over the answers held back in an envelope.

'What was he after?' Keeper said impatiently.

'A *samizdat*.'

'Plain talk. What's a . . .?' The word hadn't even registered.

Parritt bent over and unsnapped the latches on his attaché case. Slipping his hand inside, he brought out a large piece of paper and handed it to Keeper.

It was poor-quality paper, about the size of a page of tabloid newspaper. A photograph was glued in the upper left corner. There were dried splotches of glue in the other corners. Other pictures had evidently been removed from here. Stamped in the empty spaces were the words 'ON FILE' and long identification numbers. Looking closely, Keeper saw that the remaining photograph was a typewritten page of Russian words. Their arrangement indicated that the subject matter was a poem. Even for those who could read the language, it would be an ordeal to decipher; the typewriting job was badly botched, and the picture was out of focus, streaked by incompetent developing.

'What is it?' asked Keeper.

'An example of "samizdat". That's Russian slang, a composite of their words for "Do-It-Yourself-Publishing-Company".' Parritt extended his hand for the specimen to be returned. When he had replaced it in his case and snapped the latches, he continued. 'Samizdat is the only way that any literature hostile to the Soviet regime can be reproduced and circulated inside Russia. There isn't a single printing press that isn't government controlled, not even a mimeograph is legally permitted in private hands. What I've just shown you is the people's way around the strict control. Novels, stories, poems, once they're condemned by the government as subversive, they look for an outlet through the samizdat network. Nonfiction, too: essays, criticism, histories. Technically, it's a clumsy system. Without printing presses, they have to resort to photography, typing, even hand-pressing wood blocks with each word separately carved. But somehow it works. Circulation builds by geometric progression. The author types the first finished copy and several carbons. Then he hands them out to friends who promise, in return for reading whatever he's written, to reproduce no less than two additional copies, by any method they can. The copies are passed along to others who make the same agreement. Like a chain letter. The really hot items can breed into the thousands. Sooner or later, if it merits the risks, a samizdat will be smuggled West. Roy was supposed to be on the receiving end for one of them.'

Keeper eyed Parritt dubiously. 'I've heard of books being smuggled from Russia. But I don't see Roy Keeper putting his head on the block to help. He doesn't have that kind of idealism, for one thing. In the second place, the risks would be unnecessary. Since copies can be made, the book could be mailed out, even page by page if need be; there's a limit to how much mail can be checked. Or someone travelling out could hide the pages in their luggage, the linings of clothes. Anyone willing to take the risk of meeting Roy would've taken the same risks alone.'

51

Parritt nodded. 'It works exactly that way most of the time. But this was a special case. The book involved hadn't ever been freely passed around. Only a few copies were made, and our sources say that most of those were hunted down and destroyed by the KGB. Whoever was behind the plan to use Roy must have thought it offered a better chance of getting one copy through to safety.'

'What is this paper bombshell?' Keeper asked, still unable to believe that nothing more than a book could have attracted Roy's involvement.

'The title translates as *"The Mushroom Cave"*,' Parritt replied. 'It's the memoirs of Semyon Lyndushkin. Ever hear of him?'

Keeper searched the small print of memory. He had seen the name in the news several months ago. 'He died recently, didn't he?'

'In a prison camp,' Parritt confirmed. 'Actually, he died more than a year ago, but it took a long time for the news to filter through. Lyndushkin's imprisonment and mistreatment didn't set off the usual hue and cry among the Soviet intellectuals.'

Keeper remembered more now. 'A couple of his books have already been published here, two or three years ago.'

'That's right.'

'But they weren't the kind the Russians would have objected to.'

'No, they weren't,' Parritt agreed. 'In fact, they published the first one themselves. But you have to go back much farther than his first book – back about forty years – to understand what makes Lyndushkin's memoirs a threat. In the nineteen-twenties he hadn't become an author yet. He was a staunch Party man holding down a desk job in the OGPU, the secret police. A model of loyalty, efficiency and discretion, it seems; he moved up the ladder, but not so fast that anyone got jealous. Then, in the thirties, Stalin began his purges, the wholesale slaughter of anyone the boss suspected of conspiring against him. Nobody knows how many were liquidated. For the main event alone, the "great terror" between thirty-six and thirty-eight, some guesses go over a million. The secret police, by then called the NKVD, were handling the "technicalities". As if it didn't have

52

enough to do, the NKVD was also purging itself. That meant rapid advancement for Lyndushkin. Apparently he was a favourite of the secret police's head man during those years, a paranoid dwarf named Yezhov. As offices near Yezhov emptied out, Lyndushkin moved closer.

'Then one day his number came up, too. Unlike most of the others, however, Lyndushkin got out alive. Quite a trick to pull off in those days. We don't know how he managed it. He simply dropped out of sight for thirty years. When he reappeared on the scene in the Khrushchev era, the executioner had become an intellectual. He'd written a book called *The Potato Devils*. Know it?'

'I've heard of it,' Keeper said.

'It's a mild satire,' Parritt explained, 'about a Russian Orthodox priest in a peasant village. His congregation is shrinking under Party pressure against religion, so he quits, becomes a bureaucrat, and winds up commissar of a vodka distillery. It's funny, well-written, but hardly strong stuff. Under Khrushchev, censorship had relaxed enough so that *The Potato Devils* got the seal of approval. But in 1964, after Khrushchev fell from power, Lyndushkin was put on trial. The charges hinged on his novel, but that was only an excuse. Since he'd reformed, they were afraid he'd write a detailed worm's-eye view of the purges, the inside story. To prevent him, they put him away. The samizdat network was evolving at that time, and if those memoirs had been circulated and had got through to the West, the propaganda value to us would have been immeasurable. Anybody in Russian politics who came through the thirties alive had to be knifing somebody else in the back. The only way to prove their own loyalty was to betray somebody else. Which means there's blood on the hands of the men who are on top now – some of them, anyway. They're just the men – the ones who were assistants then in the smallest back rooms – that Lyndushkin's memoirs would spotlight. The Government knew before Lyndushkin's trial that if the book did get to the West it had to be a blockbuster. His first book had already become a best-seller here, based on the critical acclaim. Add to that the special appeals of a political thriller, historical interest, morbid curiosity, a growing mystique about the author –'

Keeper interrupted, 'I still don't see how any tremendous damage would've been done. We know about the purges. Khrushchev himself has written up the details.'

Parritt shook his head. 'We may know there were purges, we may know the names of the big men who were eliminated, or who cracked under the pressure and killed themselves. But we don't know very much about how the survivors survived. Judging from the fear the Soviet regime has of Lyndushkin's book, there's at least one man at the top, or very near it, who could come out a common murderer if the story was told. That's not the kind of report any man would like millions of people to read, let alone a man partly responsible for controlling a major world power.

'As for the Khrushchev book,' Parritt went on quickly, 'you may recall there were doubts about its authenticity. Many experts thought it had been cooked up and delivered into our hands by the KGB. If so, it may have been intended as insurance against Lyndushkin's inside story. Khrushchev didn't provide any really new details. Comb through his references to the purge, and you find the blame placed firmly and totally on Stalin. The only other people who come off looking bad are already dead; and Khrushchev himself owned up to a bit of skulduggery. It does seem possible, therefore, that this was a strategy to undercut any future publications naming names. The KGB itself might have stirred up doubts about the authenticity of Khrushchev's memoirs, to prime Westerners to remember that any book coming out of Russia may be a fake.'

'But why bother?' said Keeper. 'They put Lyndushkin away, silenced him.'

'They put him away,' Parritt acknowledged, 'except that three years after he went to Siberia another Lyndushkin book came West. Somehow he'd found the time, the materials, a channel to pass it along. Still, it wasn't the book we were hoping for. This one was about some labour camp prisoners who try to organize an orchestra – Lyndushkin's comment on the indomitable love of art in the human spirit. The critics called it a masterpiece.' Parritt's inflection suggested defeat. 'It was a suicide note. Once he'd shown he could write while in confinement and smuggle it out, they couldn't afford to give him another chance. He died two months after *The Orchestra* was published over here.'

'Then, when did he produce the memoirs?' Keeper said.

'Oh, he had plenty of time for that. Thirty years. It was probably the first thing he wrote.'

'Wait a second. That doesn't add up. If he had this book on hand, why would he keep sending out the others?'

'Look, because these Russian writers are hounded by the regime, that doesn't mean they don't love their country. Lyndushkin may have had trouble deciding whether or not to release the memoirs, felt they might be too damaging. Add that he couldn't have written them without doing a certain amount of character assassination on himself. How could he say who was murdering who without admitting he was an accomplice? He probably didn't look forward to living that down; so he gave the book to friends to keep until after his death.'

'A year ago,' Keeper noted. 'It's still taken a long time to come out.'

Parritt seemed weary of Keeper's scepticism. 'I can't give you all the answers. I might know more if we'd handled this operation. But the Red literary crowd isn't panting to deal with Americans on my level. Samizdats come out through a web of personal contacts, usually via the French or Italians. Strictly amateurs. They work slowly.'

Now at last it began to ring true for Keeper. He couldn't imagine Roy investing himself in an ideological struggle. But if Roy had gotten mixed up with amateurs, the adventure might have been undertaken more on a dare, for a friend. And they wouldn't have cared what his background was; there would have been no rigorous screening process.

He stood and walked around the room. Again Parritt swivelled his chair to hold Keeper always in his frontal view.

'It's starting to fit,' Keeper muttered, 'from Roy's end. He went in on this noble effort to save freedom of the press, and muffed it. But why is the other side throwing in all the mumbo-jumbo about espionage? Why elevate this amateur job to a pro operation?'

Parritt was still sitting with hands folded neatly in his lap, like a small boy who had been carefully instructed in how to behave. 'The reason for that goes beyond the importance of Lyn-dushkin's book by itself. I've told you how effective the samiz-dat network has been in circumventing the repression of criticism. As we analyse it, the Russians have finally decided that the weakest link may be the conscience of the intellectuals, the very thing that inspires their opposition to the regime. The Government thinks it can turn that conscience against itself – by proving that we're willing to employ our espionage appara-tus to bring out a book. Many dissident writers would then be disinclined to nourish the samizdat system. They'd muzzle themselves rather than be used as political pawns. Some, of course, would nevertheless continue speaking out. But if the case against Roy was proven, anyone involved in samizdat activity would be easier to prosecute in the future.'

'I don't see there have been any problems in the past,' Keeper said. 'They imprisoned Lyndushkin easy enough. And a lot of others.'

'But the Government moves reluctantly every time,' Parritt said. 'It's hard to make charges of disloyalty stick against men like Pasternak and Solzhenitsyn. The feeling these men have for their country is too clearly expressed in what they've written. Every time the Kremlin silences men like that it takes a risk of being called the less constant lover, the greater enemy of the people. Roy's case will establish a precedent: that we're ready to work just as hard to bring home an idea or some notes on history, as a set of plans for their top-secret weapon. That would provide a solid legal footing for charging any dissident author with treason.'

Keeper realized now there were answers for everything. It had all been thought out, analysed. Parritt's voice, the flat dis-passionate manner in which he discussed the passions and com-mitments of other men, was the voice of the computer, the machine behind him. It did more than certify his credentials; it had chosen the man who carried them, programmed him with all the facts.

'The Russians have so far concealed the very thing you say they're hot to prove,' Keeper observed. 'There hasn't been a word about Lyndushkin in connection with Roy.'

'There's a theatrical turn to the Russian character,' Parritt said, 'very useful when angling for world opinion. They plan their news bulletins for maximum effect, to grab a different headline every day. Rest assured their story will come out, piece by piece. As each lie is told we'll react accordingly.'

Accordingly, Keeper thought. His impatience had left him. He looked on Parritt as an extension of the computer, to be played like an instrument. Push the right button and the answer came out. There was just one more button. This was the main one, Keeper felt, certainly where Roy was concerned. 'At what point do you accordingly take the screws off the newspapers?' he asked. 'Let them print what they know about Roy . . .?'

There was a silence.

'Come on, Parritt,' Keeper rasped, 'you people aren't amateurs. You'd let Roy be smeared soon enough if it suited your plans.' He moved up on Parritt. 'So when does it happen? Why are you holding back his record? You've got everything to gain by making this espionage charge look ridiculous.' Keeper heard in his own voice not so much an argument, but a plea. He had a feeling that Roy was going to be abandoned. And suddenly, seeing his own callousness mirrored in Parritt's pragmatic analysis, Keeper hated himself for it. 'You're helping the Russians make their case,' he added. 'Why, Parritt? Why?'

Parritt hesitated. 'A Russian student who was supposedly your son's contact has also been arrested. He and Roy will probably stand trial together. Students like this boy have played a key role in the dissident movement in Russia. The authorities never fail to crack down hard. That doesn't make us feel good, but there is nevertheless something to be salvaged out of the situation. We can make our own pitch for world opinion based on the Kremlin's brutality to these young crusaders. However, if it were known they were linked up with a druggie, a draft-dodging dropout, they might get confused in some minds with all the other irresponsible hippies. The Russian crackdown could be put on a basis that even the most rabid anti-Communists would understand. And we'd lose a valuable source of propaganda.'

'Propaganda?' Keeper echoed hotly. 'That's a Nazi word, for God's sake.'

'Latin,' Parritt replied evenly.

'Jesus,' Keeper hissed, 'you don't even know what you're fighting any more. You're supposed to be against a system that represses free distribution of news and opinion. And how do you fight it? By resorting to censorship. You're all balled up, Parritt. You've got the priorities all wrong. To save the image of these kids you'll let a case be made against them that will undermine that samizdat business they've worked for.'

Parritt was unruffled. 'These are hard decisions to make, Keeper. We do the best we can. We're happy as long as we keep things on this battlefield – opinions, images, preferences of the mind and heart, where money and words are the weapons, not bomb.'

'You're happy, great.' Keeper stepped towards Parritt, hovered over the chair, his fists clenched threateningly. 'And meanwhile you bastards let Roy take the rap.'

Parritt glared up at Keeper. 'It's our business to save lives in the millions, not one at a time.' He bent down quickly, picked up his attaché case and rose to his feet. 'I've told you what it's all about, Keeper. Now that you understand, we're hoping you won't make trouble.'

He stood as if waiting for an answer from Keeper, an assurance of support.

Keeper said nothing.

'I swear to you,' Parritt went on, 'you'll only be hurting your son.' He waited another moment, then turned, walked to the door, and let himself out.

Insurance

Keeper had finished opening the mail. There were, in all, three telegrams from Captain Randolph Sealing of the Wyoming State Police. Earlier, Keeper had found the second of the series. The first was the same minus the word 'AGAIN'; the third had added the word 'URGENT'. They had been sent one each day, starting four days ago. Then the emergency had evaporated. There had been no telegram yesterday, none today. Still, the coincidence of the telegrams with Roy's capture aroused Keeper's curiosity.

An answering drawl at the other end of the line said, 'State Police, Overton Barracks'. Keeper asked to be put through to Sealing. 'Sorry, sir, the captain is on vacation.'

'This is Jack Keeper. I've had three telegrams asking me to call.'

The reaction was immediate. A new extension clicked on.

'Handlebar,' said a deep voice.

'What?' A password?

'Lieutenant Willis Handlebar. What can I do fer ya?'

Keeper visualized him by the name, a brawny frontiersman with a curled droopy moustache.

'This is Jack Keeper. I've received some telegrams –'

'Yes sir, we know about that, sir. It's all cleared up.'

'What is?'

The line was dead for a couple of seconds. Keeper thought he had been cut off. But then Handlebar came on again. 'Burglary it was. Some jewellery taken from your wife's house – ex-wife, I mean – over at Silverbend . . .'

'What's that got to do with me?'

'Insurance. Your wife not bein' around, they asked us to call you for a list of anything you'd gave her. But it's all recovered now. Everything's tied up neater'n a schoolmarm's bustle.'

Keeper was looking vacantly out the window; a slight haze of smog floated over the city's skyline. Hearing the Westerner's quaint expression made him feel connected to another time as much as another place.

He thanked Handlebar and hung up. For the true reason behind the telegrams he would have to try somewhere else. The newspaper story reporting Susan's departure from Wyoming had appeared two days ago; therefore she had not left home when the last telegram was sent.

Wyoming Information gave out Sealing's home number, and Keeper dialled direct. A woman answered. Keeper asked for Sealing without giving his own name. There was the rustic clatter of a screen door slamming, the woman's voice faintly calling, 'Randy!' and, a full minute later, Sealing came on.

'Sorry t'keep ya,' the voice said heartily. 'Been shoein' my horse. Who's this?'

'Jack Keeper. I'm calling from New York – about those telegrams.'

'Why're you callin' here?' The voice had gone cold.

'I called the barracks first. They said those telegrams were sent to get information about stolen jewellery. I know that's a lie.'

Keeper heard the policeman breathing, a low wheezing sound like wind whistling in through the screen door.

'All right, mister,' Sealing said finally. 'I'll tell it to ya once, straight through, then I'm hangin' up. I figger you got a right to know, no matter who says different. But if it gets out I told ya, the next lay-off ain't gonna be with pay. So don't never say where you heard. Savvy?'

'I understand,' Keeper said.

Another loud deep inhale. 'Five days back, early mornin', one of our patrols seen a car wreck. It was down in the valley off Thunderbird, a mountain hereabout. Way up on the road a fence was sheared through. Car musta gone off during the night, exploded in the valley. It was burnt black, still smokin' when we got to it. There was a body in it. That hadn't lasted the fire so good as the car; couple of charred bones was all. Didn't seem no way of makin' identification. Ya see, the licence plates on the car was missin'. Well, we thought first they could've melted, looked to be a real hot fire. But the men up in the state crime lab, they said there hadn't been no plates on the car. Same folks got us a serial number off the motor block. That's how we traced the car to Mrs Keeper.

'I started with the telegrams then. Wanted to ask for any X-rays and such you might dig up from doctors or dentists – to help us make sure about the remains.'

'And that's what got you sidelined?' Keeper put in.

'I'm tellin' it, mister. Just hang on!'

The policeman had been under quite a strain, Keeper thought, to be on such a short fuse. He was about to apologize for the interruption, but the voice came on again, harsher, edgier, grabbing sharp breaths at closer intervals.

'I kept up wirin' you 'til I heard your wife had left here alive and well, day after the accident – while we was still workin' on who owned the car. If I'd left things there, it woulda been fine. But it didn't half seem to me that she was runnin' out on somethin' shady. So I sent on to Washington, where she was by then; said she was wanted for questioning. Oh, I knew she was there 'cause of what happened with your boy, but you don't let people get away with murder just 'cause you feel sorry for 'em. That's what I thought anyway. But somebody sure thought different. Word come right down from the Governor that the investigation was closed. And my vacation started right then. That's all I know. I'm cuttin' off now. Just you don't forget your part of the bargain.'

The receiver went silent, deader than a seashell. Keeper lowered it slowly into the cradle, but his hand stayed on it, gliding over the ebony plastic.

There had been a time when he would have dismissed immediately any suspicion of Susan. But what did he know of her now, what she had become, what grudges might have been born in their years apart? Only a few hours earlier he had thought Roy was a purposeless dupe. Nothing was certain any more. The dust of assumptions that had lain undisturbed for many years had been gusted into a murky whirl by the opening of a door.

She was capable of killing, he recalled. Being raised on a ranch had bred in her the responses of a pioneer. They had been hunting together several times, and she had been good, unafraid of guns, with no squeamishness about shooting the animals most women gave a cooing sympathy – rabbit, deer, birds. Her taste for the sport was one reason she had gone back to live in Wyoming after the divorce. If that much of the frontier code was part of her, perhaps it was a small step to personally settling some bitter grudge with a killing. She might have seized the circumstances of Roy's arrest as an ideal opportunity, realizing the authorities would place a mantle of protection around her to ensure co-operation. Keeper thought of the letter he had received from her, the bitter tone he had thought unlike her. It would be understandable if, at the time she wrote it, she had been coming down from an unbalanced fury.

Without any awareness of leaving the apartment, Keeper found himself in the elevator going down. It was almost as if some instinct were moving him. Self-preservation? Could he have asked for his phone to be disconnected in the same way? Without awareness, to save himself, keep himself out of it.

The elevator man turned to Keeper, his eyes round and bright like the buttons on his control panel.

'Terrible thing about your son, Mr Keeper. Hope he'll be all right. I'll light a candle for him.'

'Do that,' Keeper said.

The operator faced into the corner again.

There were no reporters or photographers outside the building. Was he milked out already, the only sensations he could provide stale and redundant? Or were there further instructions to leave him alone?

A cab pulled up at the kerb. The doorman opened the yellow door. But looking into the vehicle, at the 'where to?' expression on the driver's face, Keeper realized he had nowhere to go. No one waited for him, nowhere would his unexpected arrival be a happy surprise. He shook his head and walked away from the taxi. Across the street was the park. Its bright autumn might paint over the gloom. He dared his way into the traffic, and crossed over.

He saw the expected sights. Small children sailing boats, scampering past KEEP OFF THE GRASS signs chased by starched governesses; double-file lines of older children on school excursions; horses being cantered along the bridle path by their riders. Today he felt it was all false, not a carefree romp, but a sedulous effort to imitate some etching of another era. At sunset the revel would end, the park would empty out, gaiety genuflect unquestioning to fear. It was astounding what people could accept now without protest. Did anyone boycott the park because violent deaths occurred there? It was accepted, dismissed as the toll of modern life. Bodies turned up at dawn behind the same bushes where young daylight commandos had played war games.

How much, Keeper wondered, was he accepting blindly that in another time he would have questioned, found intolerable? He sat down on one of the benches lining an asphalt path.

The most recently added part of the puzzle came first to mind: Sealing's story. One thing was undeniable. An attempt had been made to conceal the victim's identity. That did point to murder. If Susan had not done it, then who? And why had her car been the instrument? Whose body had been reduced to a few blackened bones . . .?

Keeper bolted upright. Going over Sealing's narrative, he saw one place where truth might have been side-tracked. The policeman's original motive for contacting Keeper had been to obtain positive means of identifying the body as Susan's. Once the car had been established as hers, she would be assumed the victim. That line of reasoning had only been ruled out when Sealing had learned Susan was alive. But how had he learned? He had, he said, 'heard' it. The information had been passed along. From newspaper accounts? Parritt's briefing had given an insight into the matter-of-fact way in which print could be controlled – if the national interest was deemed at stake.

No. Keeper swerved away from the idea. Tried to assemble alternatives.

But the idea stayed. He took the crumpled photocopy of her letter from his pocket and read through it again. Once more the tone struck him as off-key. His eyes went to the letterhead.

Then he was on his feet running, running across a large field through scrimmaging football teams. Forebearingly, they held their play as he passed through; they were used to these interruptions, the lunchtime exercise of tired businessmen obeying doctor's orders to build up their ageing vulnerable hearts.

Soap

It had been somebody's brainstorm to make the Barony Hotel a place where guests might imagine themselves temporary courtiers in a medieval castle. On every wall and in every corner of the lobby there were suits of armour, braziers, torch fittings, coats of arms and heraldic fittings. The bars and restaurants in the lobby had been named 'The Moat Room', 'Portcullis', 'Agincourt'. It was the junkyard of Camelot – chivalry not merely dead but mummified. The loud jovial choruses of midwestern businessmen passing on their way to convention seminars seemed unaffected by the management's desire to dub them each knight-for-a-day.

For all its bogus adornments, however, the place reminded Keeper that he was undertaking to lay a siege. If Susan had not been here, he would have to batter hard to get at the truth. A convincing impression of her presence could have been easily arranged. The lobby of a hotel this size was consistently bustling with crosscurrents of arrival and departure. Any woman could be hustled to an elevator behind a shielding screen of men, and the onlookers, mostly out-of-towners, would cherish the belief that they had witnessed a molecule of history. With no more than a flurry of whispers to inform them – 'It's that woman whose son' – they would swear later they had seen her. A repetition of the masquerade could establish her departure. And in the interim a shadow could be locked in a room to which only a few knowing officials were given access. It was possible that none of the hotel's employees had seen the woman clearly enough to describe her. And even if they had, how could Keeper check their description against a mental picture of a woman he had not seen for eight years? Perhaps her hair was greying, or she had dyed it a new shade; had gained weight, or lost it. Standing in the mock-medieval hall, Keeper realized the hundred small changes that could make the most accurate description of her a contradiction of his memory. A picture would help, a snapshot. But he had none. Susan had sent him a share of the candids they had amassed, but a few weeks after his second marriage his new wife had come across them. She had teased him spitefully into a ritual exorcism of old loves, and the photographs had burned while they drank a champagne toast to their own promising future.

It seemed unlikely that he would be able to prove whether or not Susan had really been at the hotel. But he had to try. Nothing would be learned by demanding further explanations from Parritt or his superiors. The suspicions he had now went beyond anything that could be excused by the necessities of image-making propaganda.

The desk clerk had fully absorbed the spirit of his surroundings. He regarded Keeper with the disdain of a feudal lord receiving petition from a serf.

'I'd like a room,' Keeper said.

The clerk pushed over a register.

'A particular room,' Keeper explained.

One half the clerk's pencil moustache lifted like an inquisitive eyebrow. The rest of his face remained frozen.

'You had a guest at the hotel,' Keeper continued. 'Susan Keeper. I'd like the same room she occupied.'

The thin line of hairs over the clerk's mouth dropped back in place. Inexplicably, he leaned over the counter and scanned the floor at Keeper's feet, then straightened up. Again his moustache curled with curiosity. 'No camera? Or is it just a statement you want? Well, I'll tell you what I've told the rest. Mrs Keeper rested here yesterday evening for several hours after arriving from Washington. That's all I know.'

Judging from the clerk's tired cadences, it was a set speech he had given more than a few times. There was also a tarnished familiarity about the way he closed his hand around the twenty-dollar bill Keeper held out.

It was a suite, 3511 A and B. With his first glimpse into the rooms as the bellboy pushed open the door, Keeper realized afresh that his investigation was hopeless. The rooms – a sitting room and bedroom – were perfectly in order, cleaned in preparation for the next guest. What could possibly remain of any clues? He went through the motions, though; looking into closets, probing the crevices of furniture, stripping the bed, lifting the mattress, turning back the carpets, inspecting the bathroom. Until he decided the search was over and sat down to rest, he wasn't aware of the extent of his frustration. Then around him he saw the shambles, as if a violent brawl had taken place. He laughed to himself; it wasn't every guest that booked a room merely to tear it apart.

What else could he do . . .?

Someone responsible for servicing the room could have seen something. The hall maid. He started for the phone, but as he saw the mess from new angles thought it better not to send for the maid. She would either be antagonized by the amount of work he'd created for her; or retreat, fearing he was in a frenzy. He left the suite and walked around the corridors until he found the linen closet. A small old woman was sitting inside on a fold-down chair, an open can of beer in one hand, an open Bible in her lap. She lifted her head slowly when Keeper greeted her. Her vacant eyes seemed, like the sheets and pillowcases in her care, to have been bleached, sent out too often to a stringent laundry.

She answered his questions without hesitation, without concern.

No, she had not seen anyone in the room, but her shift began at eight in the morning and ended at four in the afternoon. Yes, the room had definitely been used last night. This morning she had found the ashtrays full of cigarettes and cigars, the bed rumpled, some empty drinking glasses on the sitting-room tables, and many newspapers lying in chairs and on the floor. With stern disapproval she noted that among the papers had been a racing form.

It added up to an impression of one or two men assigned to guard Susan's privacy, killing time while she napped in the bedroom.

Keeper had thanked the maid and started away when she called after him to add one more thing, a small detail that struck her as unusual: None of the towels had been used, and none of the complimentary packages of soap had been opened.

It was, Keeper believed, small but not trivial. Wouldn't a woman under stress, having already done a considerable amount of travelling and facing another long journey, take a moment to freshen herself, wash her face, do her make-up?

The deduction seemed elementary until he was back amid the chaos of the suite. The disorder around him challenged the order of his mind, his thinking. Was it reasonable to perceive sinister conspiracies because a package of soap hadn't been opened?

Still, even if she had been at the hotel, there were other mysteries left unexplained. The car wreck and Roy's capture had to be linked by more than coincidence of time. Higher powers had intervened in both cases to bury the facts.

But as long as he kept his detached position, stayed on the sidelines, Keeper's theory would never be more than a vision of vague outlines. To test it, to see the design clearly, he would have to leave his safe place, follow her route and Roy's. And there was something more than a trial of logic moving him, something stronger than outrage at being lied to, manipulated. There was a longing, an almost animal need to know that she was safe. He feared her death as an omen that what he had known with her, not that one love alone, but the very ability to love, could never be recaptured.

Not to demonstrate a concern for her, nor to win her back, but simply to preserve some faith in his own future, Keeper felt he must find her alive.

'Wait there, just wait right there!'

Fall had listened patiently through Keeper's account of the conversation with Sealing and his cursory hotel investigation. But when Keeper announced his next move, the lawyer cut in with his directive and banged down the phone. Ten minutes later, Fall knocked on the door of Suite 3511 A and B. As Keeper opened the door, Fall's glance shot past him to the over-turned furniture and scattered bedding.

'Let's have a drink downstairs,' Fall said quickly. 'Not very conducive here to an orderly discussion.'

Keeper shrugged. On their way to the elevators, they stopped at the linen closet. The maid Keeper had spoken to had finished her shift and gone home. Her replacement reported that she knew the room had been occupied yesterday, but not by whom. Fall listened dubiously, contributing no questions of his own.

In the lobby, Fall headed for The Moat Room. They waited to enter while a scaled-down wooden drawbridge, activated by electric eye, descended to span a pool sunken in the floor.

'Cute idea,' Fall remarked.

'Not if you're thirsty,' Keeper said humourlessly.

Fall squinted at Keeper. 'It wouldn't hurt you to unwind a little, Jack.'

'You see what happens to this bridge when it unwinds,' Keeper observed. 'People walk all over it.'

Inside the room was dark, suffused by a reddish glow from simulated torches. As his eyes adjusted, Keeper saw the forms standing around the walls were not customers but suits of armour. In this place, he mused, they might be waiters. There were no other customers, but Fall headed into the farthest corner, choosing a table as if the room were jammed with eavesdroppers.

They sat in silence until the waiter had taken their order and gone away.

Then Keeper said, 'Well, Andy, you wanted me to take a fatherly interest. Now I'm ready to go all the way. Are you going to help?'

Fall drew his heavy body forward and put his elbows on the table, working to project an aura of thoughtfulness. 'Jack, I think you should be concerned, naturally. But this trip, it's a mistake. I mean, if you go for the wrong reasons.'

'I can't think of better reasons than the ones I've got. Something rotten is at the centre of this, and I'm the only one who cares.'

'The average man isn't equipped to make judgements about these things, Jack.'

'The news is being controlled here, Andy. Can't you make a judgement on that?'

Fall shrugged. 'Managing the news isn't a diabolical innovation. In one form or another it's done every day. If it's in the national interest to hold something back, then it's done. We have to accept that.'

'We're not talking just about holding things back now. This is something new with Susan. There's a possibility that she's dead and a different story is being handed out.'

'That's preposterous,' Fall huffed.

'Then what do you make of the policeman's story?'

Fall hesitated. 'I didn't actually hear the story . . .'

Keeper's eyes bored through the red darkness. 'Meaning what?'

Fall realized that what he had implied could ignite Keeper's raw temper. He tacked appeasingly. 'I only meant, well, that I might interpret the facts better if I'd heard his actual words. That's my legal training.'

'You're not doubting that Sealing did tell me —'

'No, no,' Fall insisted. 'But don't forget, in almost the same breath you passed the story along to me, you said the man would deny it if I checked.'

'Because he's afraid,' said Keeper quickly. 'I don't care if you check, but it's a dead end. That cop had enough initiative to talk once. Now he's done his duty. Next time anyone asks about it he'll swear up and down he never talked to me, that he's spent every minute shoeing his goddam horse.'

The waiter brought the drinks and disappeared again into the gloom.

Fall took a long pull from his martini, then said:

'All right, take the story apart. The car went halfway down a mountain and burned in a fire so hot the police thought the licence plates had melted. That could have screwed up the serial number on the motor. It took the crime lab to read it off anyway. Maybe they got it wrong. Maybe the car wasn't Susan's. Even assuming that it was, you can't rule out an accident.'

'Then, why was it left for the police to discover? Why wasn't it reported?'

'No one spotted the wreckage, I suppose.'

'That would explain it,' Keeper admitted, 'if Susan had been in the car. But if she wasn't, if she were alive, wouldn't she report her own car missing?'

Fall gave no ground. 'She might have lent the car to a friend, then left Wyoming before it was returned. It wouldn't have been the biggest thing on her mind at the time . . .'

69

Keeper listened with rising disgust to Fall's interpretations. What if he pointed out that Sealing had been disciplined for pursuing his inquiries, what innocent reasoning would Fall produce then? That Sealing had been punished for blundering insensitivity, unfairly harassing a woman who was coping with another, more tragic problem? If one wanted to look at the incident with a blameless eye, perhaps any part of it could be glossed over. But Keeper had heard Sealing's voice. The policeman had sounded too indignant, too wounded by being muzzled and put out to pasture for Keeper to believe it was deserved.

It was useless, though, to press Fall further on hearsay. Keeper took out the letter and tossed it on the table.

Fall finished sucking the red heart out of an olive, dropped the rest into his glass.

'What's this?'

'Susan's letter, the copy.'

'Yes. I should have mentioned that – dead women don't write letters.'

Keeper unfolded the paper. 'Read it.'

'I have.'

'Read it again,' Keeper commanded. 'Out loud.'

Fall flashed a petulant glance at Keeper, then picked up the copy. Straining to pick out the words through the darkness, he read slowly in a belittling singsong: 'Dear Jack, I couldn't get to you by phone, so I'm writing. For what –'

'That's enough,' Keeper interrupted. 'That first sentence.'

Fall was draining his glass. 'Perfectly straightforward,' he said in a garble, his tongue wrestling with the olive.

'*Too* perfectly. It's the reason for this letter, the thing that gives it validity. She wouldn't have written if my phone had been working. But then we wouldn't have this handy proof that she's alive. With the phone dead, the letter became necessary.'

Fall shook his head. 'Jack, you're –'

Keeper rode over him. 'Look at how attention was drawn to it. Even before I'd seen the letter, you did, and half a dozen newsmen. Witnesses. It would be hard to find witnesses to a simple phone call.' Keeper grabbed the letter, shoved it closer to Fall's face. 'Would you swear that's her handwriting?'

Fall knocked Keeper's hand aside. 'I haven't seen Susan's

handwriting in ages. But I have some of her old letters on file. Handwriting characteristics don't change much. If it makes you feel better, go to an expert, take an old sample and this letter –'

'This copy, you mean. Who ran it through the machine, Andy?'

'One of the men who brought the original.'

'A secretary could have done just as well.'

'Well, he asked for the machine and I –'

With a knowing nod, Keeper broke in: 'He was a little careless, have you noticed? The copy is slurred, as if it moved a bit during the process. Still, suppose some expert should declare it a forgery. How much weight would that carry if he wasn't working from the original – that precious original we don't have.'

'God, Jack, if you want to put a Machiavellian slant on everything, go ahead. Who the hell could ever stop you? But don't expect me to chime in. I won't sling this kind of mud to please you, even if it means my job.' Fall's voice had risen to a shout.

It was very quiet in the bar. The bartender, who had been stacking clean glasses, had stopped and was staring across the room. A few seconds went by, then the sound of clinking glass resumed.

Keeper said, his voice low, 'You've got it wrong, Andy. I don't want to make any wild accusations. All I want you to do is put in this request. If I do it myself, it would be harder to explain my big change of heart. But you could say you talked me into it – that I don't want to go, but you think it's my responsibility. If they hem and haw, we'll rethink it. If you're right, though, they'll let me make the trip. I can meet up with Susan and see I was wrong.'

'They'll let you make the trip,' Fall said emphatically. 'But what then? Frankly, Jack, you may not be up to it. You can't wade into a situation like this without having a firm grip on yourself. And let's face it, the last couple of months –'

One of Keeper's hands flew off the table and clenched around the lapel of Fall's jacket. 'I'll say it once, Andy: I've been through some rough times lately, but that hasn't turned me into a mental cripple. Anything that comes my way, I can handle it.'

'I ... I'm sorry, Jack.' Fall tugged his collar back into shape as Keeper retracted his hand. 'Let's go up to your room,' he added. 'I'll call from there.'

The glass of whisky Keeper hadn't touched he now drank at a swallow. Then he paid the bill.

On the way from the bar, Fall stopped at one of the armour figures and inspected it. Keeper wondered if Fall wasn't peering through the helmet's metal visor, making sure that no one was inside listening.

Confession

The room was clean. The paint was not peeling. The windows were barred, but immense compared with the slit in the wall of his cell. Enough daylight came in so that the naked bulbs hanging from the high ceiling were not burning. Roy took a deep breath; the air was stale, but it did not stink. Gratefully savouring the small differences, he responded slowly to the man sitting at the table that all but filled the long narrow room.

The man stood, crushed out his cigarette in an ashtray. He had the build of an underweight wrestler, sturdy but not too thick. His face was pleasant and open despite a nose that was slightly off-centre, as if it had once been broken. He held out his hand.

'Mr Keeper, I'm Peter Holman.'

An unmistakably American accent. Roy focused on the man. He had expected to be confronted again with someone from KGB, to be threatened as by Schub. Two days ago? Was that all? Trying to orient himself in time, Roy almost missed what Holman was saying.

'... from Moscow, the Embassy ...'

Now Roy rushed to seize the outstretched hand. Holman nodded sympathetically at the eager lunging grip.

'I thought they'd never ...' Roy slid into a chair across from Holman.

'We've been trying to see you since the arrest,' Holman said. 'But they're usually slow giving permission, even in less serious cases. I've waited weeks to see a tourist who was locked up for failing to declare a camera at Customs.'

'How long' – Roy paused, embarrassed by the need to ask – 'how long have I been here?'

Holman gave him a searching look. 'Three days. How are they treating you?'

Roy smiled feebly. 'Like one of the family.'

'We lodged a protest when we heard you were in here,' Holman said grimly. 'The place is infamous, but it's the only prison in Batumi, and they do have the right to keep you in prison.' He took out a pack of cigarettes, offered it to Roy.

Roy shook his head. 'Can't you get me out of this?'

Lighting a cigarette for himself, Holman couldn't answer before Roy went on. 'I know you must be doing everything possible. But I'm going nuts here. You can't imagine what it's like.' He flung his hands across the table, a plea and an attack. 'How much more do I have to take?'

'That depends on you more than us,' Holman replied. From the litter of papers spread before him on the table, papers he'd been studying when Roy entered, Holman pulled out one sheet and scanned it silently.

Roy tried to read it upside down. The sun streaming through the window over his shoulder fell on the paper, made it a stinging white. Black letters vaguely shimmered through; Cyrillic letters, Roy thought. His eyes went up to Holman's face: heavy features, dark-brown eyes, coarse black hair. Was he really from the Embassy? Schub had looked more American.

Holman kept looking at the paper. 'You know how serious the charges are ...?'

'They said they'd make it look like I came in a sub. Are they really peddling that shit?'

'They've released pictures, two sailors from the patrol boat holding up the raft you were captured in.'

Roy's hands contracted to fists and slammed down on the table. The door of the room opened, and the guard posted outside peered in, glanced from Roy to Holman, then ducked out.

'You've got to get hold of yourself, man,' Holman urged, 'or you won't be able to help me; and that means helping yourself.'

'But it's not true. There wasn't any raft.' Roy slumped back on his chair. How much more should he tell Holman? If the Embassy knew everything would they still help, put their prestige on the line? Maybe they thought his only crime was illegal entry. 'I was in a fishing boat I'd rented for the day,' he said.

'What happened to it?'

'The Russians sank it when they picked me up.'

Holman looked silently at Roy.

'You believe me, don't you?'

'It doesn't matter what I believe. This case is going through their courts. If they want to put you away for ten years, they can do it.'

Ten years. The words had a tangible force; like a punch in the gut, they momentarily robbed Roy of breath. He eyed the package of cigarettes on the table, sorry he'd turned one down. It would make a bribe for a guard. Christ! they had him thinking like a convict already.

Holman was shuffling again through his papers. He picked one out and slid it over to Roy. 'Seen one of these?'

Roy glanced at it. 'One. I've seen dozens.'

'We want you to sign it.'

Roy stared unbelievingly at Holman.

'That's what I'm here to tell you,' Holman continued. 'This confession has to be signed.'

Roy studied the sheet in front of him more carefully. Where the previous copies had said 'IN SPECIFIC', this had the more correct English, 'SPECIFICALLY'. Otherwise, it was exactly the same wording as was already etched in his memory. He lifted his eyes again to Holman's face. The nose that had been broken could have given it a muggish, dishonest aspect. Instead, it seemed to enhance an impression of solidity, the mark of a man who had fought sometime for something he believed in.

'How can you want me to sign this?' Roy asked quietly.

Holman took a puff of his cigarette, drew his lips back and sucked air as if the inside of his mouth were burning. 'We're not asking you to admit anything you haven't really done.'

So they did know, Roy thought. 'But still, it's giving them something to build that phony case on. Any confession helps them.'

'It helps everyone,' Holman said. 'The Russians have offered a deal. We have someone they want back – a defector, maybe, or someone we've picked up on spy charges. I don't know who I'm not in on that. Whoever it is, an exchange is agreeable to both sides. But not until after a trial with this confession in evidence. That's part of the deal.'

It could be a KGB trick, Roy realized. His intuition that

Holman could be trusted was meaningless. There would be no spies unless trust could be manufactured. Once the confession was signed he would be at their mercy.

'What if I hold out?' Roy said. 'If there's someone the Russians want they'd still go for a trade.'

'Probably. But it might take much longer. Months instead of days.'

'Why should they wait?' Roy challenged. 'What's the point of holding on to me?'

Holman hesitated. 'I'm afraid that would be our idea, not theirs. If you go to trial on what look like trumped-up charges, we can't bring you home too fast. That would set off a bad public reaction. There are a lot of Americans moving around the world at any one time. Diplomats, businessmen, tourists. They need to know they can travel without constant fear of being grabbed and used for bait. It won't go down well with them if it looks like that happened to you and we knuckled right under. That would be giving the Russians a licence to try the same thing again, anytime they were shopping for a deal. So sign the confession. Then people will know there was a good reason why you were arrested.'

'It's a frame, anyway. You know that? They set me up for this. They knew I was coming.' Roy's voice broke to an adolescent whine.

Holman nodded. 'We figured that. The most we can do about it now is let you know where you stand. If you agree to plead guilty, there will be a quick trial, within the next few days; you'll be charged and sentenced solely on what's in the confession. The prosecution has promised to leave out the fairy tales, retract them on the basis of "new evidence". As soon as the trial is over, you'll fly to Moscow and leave from there when we deliver their man. You could be home within a couple of weeks.' Holman took a last draw on his cigarette and crushed it out under his foot. 'There's no point in refusing,' he added.

No point. Roy stared at Holman's flattened cigarette butt. Around it, others dotted the floor. How many do-or-die consultations had taken place here today? Did those poor creeps on the other side of the wall get to see defence lawyers? A fat lot of good it did them. They were still here rotting. As he might be, even if he did trust Holman's advice.

'Did you hear me?' said Holman.

Roy nodded listlessly without looking up from the floor.

'Will you sign?'

Roy didn't answer.

Holman rose, came around the table and sat on it beside Roy's chair.

'Listen, if we don't agree to this deal, you'll be sent to a labour camp in Siberia. But they won't just put you there and forget about you. A month or two after you're sent away, stories will reach our correspondents that you're being ill-treated, in failing health. The stories will have more than a grain of truth; you've seen what they can do.' Holman nodded towards the wall, indicating what lay beyond. 'Those stories won't be coming out by a friendly grapevine, though. KGB will plant them, hoping to build up some pressure back home to get you released. It could work. They're a funny bunch, our citizens; they'll bitch if we bring you home too fast, and they'll write letters to their congressmen if we leave you here too long. There are a lot of terrible associations built into that one word "Siberia". And you'll be remembered as that nice boy who got a raw deal. If enough people make a fuss, eventually we'll have to make a deal anyway.'

'Then I'll wait,' Roy murmured brokenly.

'Don't be crazy,' Holman rejoined sharply. 'In the meantime you'll do anywhere from six months to six years. Hauling logs or mining salt in subzero temperatures; illclothed, housed in unheated shacks. Even at your age, your health could be permanently ruined.'

Now Roy raised his face up. He was trembling. With fear, perhaps, or anger; he didn't know which.

'Why are you pushing me so hard?' he said, smouldering.

'To save you unnecessary suffering.'

'Sweet of you. Real humanitarian.'

There was a silence. Holman stood and moved to the end of the room. 'There is a little more to it,' he admitted. He began to pace along the marginal strip of floor beyond the end of the table. Passing in and out of a shaft of sunlight that slanted across his path, he looked like an image flickering slowly on a screen. 'Now that they've got you, you're like money in the bank. Right now they have something to spend it on, and we don't mind selling. If we wait, if we give them time to browse, they could see something they like better, something we'd hate to part with. But while you're locked up, if any public pressure develops to free you, our bargaining position only gets weaker. We want to close this account now.' He stopped pacing. 'Give in, kid. You don't gain anything by holding out.'

Whoever had employed Holman, thought Roy, there was substance in what he had been given to say. The setup had been arranged so that one way or another Roy could be used. The Russians didn't need a confession to condemn him. They needed it for something else. When they had it, would they really let him go?

Or did they need it at all? It was his own people who wanted the confession signed.

Roy held out his hand. 'Lend me your pen.'

Holman didn't move, 'Sorry. I can't take the confession and hand it in. I'm just here to tell you what to do when they ask.'

'When will they?' Roy was dispirited by the anticlimax. He'd committed himself now. Why couldn't the machinery move? 'They keep shoving the words at me, but nobody ever comes to collect.'

'Don't worry,' Holman said, 'they'll come now. I'll pass along your decision through the legal channels. Your next visitor will be the Procurator – the prosecution's man – or a state-assigned defence attorney. Either way, give him the signed confession, and say you want to plead guilty.'

The guard rapped on the door, leaned in and barked at Holman in Russian. Holman answered angrily, and the guard exited without rebuttal.

'We've got another minute,' Holman said, gathering his papers. 'I don't know if they'll let me in again before the trial, but I could send in a few things. Anything you want? Books, shaving stuff? You could certainly use a shave.'

Roy's hand went to his cheek, rubbed at the growth of stubble. The abrasive scratch in his palm reminded him of a part of his existence he had forgotten, a face, externals. All he had known these past three days was the ache of desperation filling him, becoming his being.

'Prisoners get shaved once a week, if they want. They aren't allowed their own razors.' Roy moved his toes, felt the canvas lining of his sneakers. He had come to understand how the small symbol of defiance was a medal to cherish.

'And books?' asked Holman, sliding the papers into his zip case.

'Yeah, I guess. Anything to pass the time. Murder mysteries, stuff like that.'

At the door they shook hands. Then Roy made another request:

'I'd like to write a couple of letters. Can you arrange it?'

Holman replied tentatively. 'I could. But if it's anything that can wait, hold off. You could write something, thinking it's perfectly harmless; the Russians will intercept it, and maybe use it against you.'

'I just want my mother to know I'm O.K. She'll be really worried. I mean, with those pictures they're –'

'She knows all about it.' Holman smiled. 'Relax. Last I heard she was on her way to meet you in Moscow.' He opened the door and stepped into the corridor. The guard waited stolidly to lead Roy back to his cell. 'I can get her a message, if you'd like,' Holman added.

'Yeah, do that. Just tell her I'm fine. Don't let her know what this place is like.' He tried to think of something else to say, so he could stay near the clean light of the room, postpone even for seconds the next breath of stinking prison air. But now the guard was gripping his arm, tugging brusquely.

'Good-bye. Thanks.' Roy muttered. Then he was being pulled towards the heavy metal door that opened into the cell blocks.

'It won't be long,' Holman called after him, and walked off by himself in the other direction.

Arabian Nights

There had been no official resistance. None. The essential documents had been prepared and delivered within a few hours. No one came forward with warning, objections, tactical advice. The man who rode with Keeper to the airport limited himself to outlining the itinerary, and one polite caution against being drawn into a question-answer period with reporters covering the departure. 'I am making this trip to help my son through a difficult ordeal.' Facing the microphones and cameras, Keeper had said only the one phrase, then boarded the plane. The same statement was repeated verbatim to the press at London's Heathrow Airport, after which a solicitous representative from the Embassy took Keeper to breakfast. The junior diplomat, a glad-handing Missourian, didn't expand Keeper's knowledge of the affair. Professing apologetically to 'know only what I read in the papers', he diverted the conversation to opportunities for investment in Europe, evidently unaware that Keeper was no longer a captain of industry. An hour and a half after setting down in London, Keeper left on the next leg of his journey.

Fourteen hours of travelling brought the sensation of being in a mild delirium. Between periods of fitful dozing on the plane to Istanbul, he tried to remember the logic of making the trip. It eluded him. A fantasy had moved him, nothing more; otherwise he would not have been allowed to go. As the plane glided towards a landing, however, he looked down at the city below, a vision from *The Arabian Nights*. He saw the profusion of minarets pointing towards the sky as stern instructive fingers emphasizing a lesson: There were fantasies born of fact.

Again an attentive consular official appeared to shepherd him through Customs; again he added little to Keeper's information. Just one new fact: Mrs. Keeper had not passed through here;

but, the official pointed out, there were many other routes by which she could have gone.

Keeper rejected the whirlwind tour that was offered to help pass the waiting time. He wanted to sleep. A cot was found for him in the airport's emergency quarantine infirmary.

A pricking stab in his arm awakened him. He rolled over to see a Turkish steward bending over his cot, the big red cupcake of a fez on his head. The Turk was gripping Keeper's arm to jostle him awake; the needle jab had come from the excessively overgrown nail on the Turk's little finger.

Twenty minutes later, after a handshake and hearty wishes of good luck, Keeper was on a Russian plane, heading for the touchdown in Russian territory: Tbilisi.

He tried to get more sleep, but the din of four propeller motors and the discomfort of the narrow tubular steel seat kept him awake. He looked around at the other passengers. Of the eighty seats, only twenty or thirty were occupied. It surprised Keeper to see even this many, as he had been surprised to learn the flight was regularly scheduled. Trained by the phrases of another era – 'the Iron Curtain' – he thought of Russia as less accessible, sealed off. Who were these people, travelling freely between two worlds? He noticed the illuminated sign at the front of the cabin, giving the standard safety instructions in Arabic and Cyrillic. Were they all Russians and Turks? One, at least one, must be detailed to watch him.

Keeper rose into the aisle and made a slow trip up and down, inspecting the passengers. Most of the men were sleeping, a few reading. No one tried to talk over the brain-rattling noise. There was only one woman, sitting alone at the rear. As Keeper walked by, a couple of readers raised their eyes to meet his. Then a large man with shaggy grey hair like llama wool caught Keeper's sleeve and laughingly shoved a bottle of vodka into his ribs.

The woman hurried up the aisle. She had an official air, the dowdy dark-blue outfit, the hefty certitude. She unleashed a scolding barrage at the vodka drinker; a pretence of anger, Keeper suspected, for the sake of appearances. Then she turned to Keeper, her voice suddenly soft. She seemed to be offering help.

He answered that he spoke only English.

Undeterred, she said, 'Zhoornal? Koffye? Oobornya?'

Then she tried posing the questions in mime. Her hands turned the pages of an invisible magazine, her lips pursed over an imaginary cup, she rubbed her hands together as if washing them. All the passengers were looking at Keeper now, as if everyone belonged to a shadow corps assigned to report his movements. He thanked the stewardess and returned to his seat.

But she followed. 'Poadooshka!' she said loudly, her mouth snapping shut, tight and determined. Her hands mimed no interpretation. Keeper made a mental note to buy a phrase book. For now he could only shake his head.

The woman remained in the aisle next to him, observing him clinically. Keeper ignored her. Hitching himself around to use some of the adjacent empty seat, he put his head back and closed his eyes.

'Poadooshka!' she bellowed, and forcibly pushed Keeper's head forward while she crammed something behind it, something soft. Keeper opened his eyes.

'Poadooshka,' the woman purred, grimly patting the pillow. And walked away before Keeper could thank her.

He was not amused to discover the absurdity of his suspicious defensiveness. Unless he could sort out the real fears from the false, he would be lost where he was going, always misreading signs, following empty clues.

His ears had grown numb to the motors. When his head fell back against the pillow, he blacked out easily.

He looked at his watch as he left the plane. Almost midnight. Twenty-four hours since he had left New York. It felt like much more. The series of tunnels and tubes and glowing caverns through which he had moved were like interconnecting parts of a time machine transporting him across centuries. He felt ancient.

The air outside, warm and damp, heightened his sluggish torpor. Stepping onto the runway from the ramp, Keeper felt its heat through his shoes. The smells of fuel and hot rubber mingled in the air with flowery fragrances carried from somewhere beyond the concrete by a faint uncooling breeze.

A man stepped to his side from the dim fringes of the floodlit path to the terminal building.

'Rough trip?' he asked genially.

Keeper saw an athletically built man with dark hair and eyes and a nose that had once been broken.

'Peter Holman, Mr Keeper. The Embassy sent me to help you over the hurdles.'

Keeper said a perfunctory hello. They shook hands. Holman gestured into the darkness where red, white, and blue reflections of the airport lighting defined the polished surface of a black limousine.

'This way,' Holman said. 'Sorry we couldn't provide an escort all down the line; we have a manpower problem. You make connections all right?'

'Fine.'

'You look beat.'

Keeper said nothing. He was concentrating his attention on the car, the chauffeur holding open the rear door. The man was in uniform. A Russian army uniform, Keeper thought.

Holman caught the startled hesitation. 'They provided the car as a courtesy. They'll also be flying you to Batumi tomorrow. And they've arranged tonight's accommodation.'

'Courtesy,' Keeper rejoined acidly. 'And I suppose the kid gets fresh flowers every day in his cell.' He climbed into the car. The door shut behind him.

Holman had stayed outside. Keeper glanced back through the rear window and saw him arguing with a fat man wearing a trench coat and overlarge fedora. Both men had their hands on the handle of Keeper's suitcase. Holman's shouting became more heated. But the suitcase went away with the fat man.

'Courtesy broke down a little,' Holman said, as he got into the car. 'It'll be returned after a search.'

As it drove off the airfield, the car stopped briefly at a barrier manned by armed police. A second car appeared and pulled ahead, red lights on the roof winking on and off. Then the limousine was waved through. The car ahead set the pace, picking up speed as the scream of a siren rose, cleaving through the damp leaden air. The road stretched grey and empty towards a flickering lake of pale yellow, the scattered street lamps of a large city. There were no other cars on the straight road. The siren shrieked its warning at no one.

'I suppose you'd like to hear about your son,' Holman said. 'I've seen him. He's in pretty good shape, considering.'

Keeper turned. 'And his mother. How is she?'

'All right, I guess. Getting the red-carpet treatment.'

'Have you seen her, too?'

'No. She arrived after I left.'

So she *was* here, and he had been permitted to come and see for himself. He chuckled drily. It had been such a long long journey. Eight years. Flaccid with exhaustion, his mind leaked memories from odd corners. He recalled a fight, the time he had held her down on the bed until she relinquished her grip on a pair of nail scissors. 'I hope you didn't put us in the same hotel,' he said lightly. 'That's all we need now, to get locked up for disturbing the peace.'

'The arrangements should suit you fine,' Holman replied. 'Her hotel is two thousand miles from yours.'

'I thought you said she was here.'

'I said she'd arrived. In Moscow. After I'd left to come down here and see Roy.'

'And she's staying there?'

Holman nodded. 'Best thing she can do under the circumstances. In cases like this the Russians almost never allow prisoners personal visitors until after the trial. It's hardly worth the strain of coming down here just to sit by and chew her nails. Not when she'll be able to take Roy home within a day or two of the trial.' Holman saw that Keeper was stunned. 'You didn't know?'

'No. I didn't know.'

'They've offered to trade. We accepted.' Holman went on to tell as much as he knew about the exchange, the confession, his part in obtaining it, and the reasons.

He was able to supply Keeper, too, with the name of the Russian to be exchanged for Roy. It had appeared in the most recent diplomatic dispatches: Pavel Yolkin. Holman claimed to know nothing more about Yolkin than what had appeared in American newspapers at the time of his arrest. He had entered the United States five months ago, heading a trade mission to promote sales of heavy machinery, a boon of the recently warmer economic climate between the super-powers. Then, three months ago, Yolkin had been picked up and detained on espionage charges that had never been fully clarified. He had not yet been brought to trial. Despite the paucity of information, Holman could speculate on the probable nature of Yolkin's activities:

'He's one of the rank-and-file agents the Russians send in every year for general snooping. Must've been grabbed for something minor – hanging around dockyards, checking cargoes, nothing newsworthy. The case was apparently too weak to prosecute right away; the Government is taking its time to prepare carefully and ensure a conviction.'

Or else, thought Keeper, more facts were being held back.

'He must be worth something,' Keeper observed. 'His employers went to some trouble to set up this exchange.'

Holman smiled tolerantly. 'Up to eleven years of training go into a KGB operator. If we land one, big or small, they want him back. Most they get for the asking. This time it's different, this time they have to work at it. That doesn't prove Yolkin's another Rudolf Abel. He's got to be small beer or we wouldn't let him go on such easy terms.'

Keeper struggled to keep alert, catch any inconsistencies. And there had been something . . .

'Did you say most of their spies we hand back on demand?'

'Unfortunately,' Holman said, 'we have to. In the last fifteen years we've unmasked over fifty KGB plants at the U.N. alone. Lump in the haul from various embassies and consulates, and it adds up to an average of five or six a year. But they're in positions carrying diplomatic immunity, so it's almost impossible to hold them. The ones like Abel or Yolkin who come in without immunity are few and far between.'

'Why leave the umbrella home if they don't have to?'

'Since we're wise to the immunity dodge, we have a special watch on their Embassy people. The way Yolkin came in, he'd have had more freedom to circulate. Of course, it also left him liable for a long prison term once he was caught. That's why they have to work to bring him home.'

Keeper weighed these revelations against Parritt's briefing.

All the careful computer logic had somehow overlooked this possibility: The Russians had merely been fattening their catch for barter. Surely the punch-card commandos could have figured that in. Recalling the efficiency of Parritt's every word and gesture, it was hard to believe there had been any casual omissions.

'When was this deal offered?' asked Keeper.

'I couldn't say for sure. I flew down last night. I was only briefed by the Ambassador late yesterday.'

'What time?'

'It was getting dark ... must've been around five-thirty, six.'

'Six. That makes it what time in New York?'

'Eight hours earlier. Why?'

Ten, Keeper thought, ten in the morning. And when he had talked with Parritt the sun had been coming through the window, facing Fifth Avenue on its western arc. That would make it one, maybe two o'clock. Parritt's failure to mention the exchange might well have been something more than careless Kremlinology.

'Why?' Holman persisted. 'What difference does the time make?'

'Just a little,' Keeper replied bitterly. 'I left New York at midnight. There were more than a few hours when I might have been told.'

'This was high level,' Holman reasoned. 'They might not have known in New York. Who'd you talk to, State Department?'

'Is that what you are?'

Holman nodded.

'Show me your credentials,' Keeper said.

Holman handed a leather folder to Keeper. Like Parritt's, the identification card was set behind a plastic window, bore Holman's name in print and signature, and had a small picture glued to it. But on this one 'U.S. DEPARTMENT OF STATE' was clearly printed, and Holman's function was specified as 'Vice Consul'.

Keeper handed back the folder. 'The man in New York gave me a card only machines can read.'

'Oh?' Holman looked at the floor of the car. 'How'd you connect with him?'

'My lawyer told someone I wanted a briefing. This guy showed up.'

Holman nodded minutely. 'He probably did know about the deal – the offer. But I told you we couldn't have gone ahead without a confession – and I hadn't talked to Roy yet. Maybe he didn't want to build your hopes up too soon.'

No. That kind of consideration wouldn't have counted with Parritt, Keeper thought.

Holman continued, 'Or maybe they wanted you around to back me up. If Roy hadn't responded to me, you could have talked to him.'

Roy would be more likely to listen to a stranger, Keeper reflected. In any case, the best persuader would be Susan. But he had been sent, not her. Had they shunted him off to where he could not prove she was no longer alive? Keeper became aware of Holman watching hawkishly.

'My wife is a pretty gutsy dame,' Keeper said finally. 'She's very close to the kid, seen him personally through a lot of tough times. She'd want to be at the trial, near him, even if she didn't get visiting privileges.'

'That may be what she wants,' Holman responded. 'But I gather the events of the last few days have wound her up pretty tight. Well, I'm only going on hints from communiqués, but her nerves must have been in bad shape when she got to Moscow.'

'Hints. What hints?'

'She went right into seclusion. And no interviews have been allowed.'

There was a silence between them.

'She wasn't the type to fall apart,' Keeper said at last. The past tense came automatically. 'She was stronger than that.'

Holman said nothing. The facts spoke for themselves.

She had been stronger, Keeper repeated to himself. But as he looked into the night, he remembered that his own admired strength had not resisted all the pressures. And for a long time now the strains of handling Roy, and failing with him, had chipped away at Susan's spirit. Perhaps finally it had shattered.

They were closer to the city now. Occasionally there was a civilian car on the road. The siren would order it aside, revving to a higher, shriller scream.

Protocol

Was it a dream, some allegory of the unconscious: a visit to hell? There was a choking stench of sulphur, constricting his throat.

Keeper opened his eyes.

It was a bedroom fit for a pious king, sparsely furnished – the large bed, a table by the french windows, a wardrobe – but each piece was old and rare. The doors of the wardrobe were inlaid with ivory, the table had a marble top, the head and foot boards of the bed were intricately carved with oriental hunt scenes. Rolling his head back on the pillow, Keeper saw the bulge of a wooden tiger writhing on the lance of a Mongol horseman. Overhead, Byzantine angels smiled at him from the ceiling.

His mind had shut down last night. He had given up caring where he was or why. From the time the car had stopped, he had noticed only that the house was big and dark and that his bed had a rather stiff mattress.

Now he came fully awake. The sulphurous odour receded, became milder. He swung his feet to the cold marble floor and went to the windows. Outside, a balcony hung over a narrow street. He stepped onto the balcony.

The surrounding buildings were of massive stone blocks, darkened by the weather of centuries. Over the roof of a low building opposite, Keeper could see down a hillside of terraced streets to a swift-flowing river. On the far bank, the city climbed in tiers over rippling hills. Modern white buildings, square practical sins of progress, hemmed in the original medieval town which crowded along the river, old houses dark and angular, bullied to the brink by a new generation.

Judging by the activity in the street, it was early morning. A stout woman was sweeping the gutter with a twig broom. A couple of stall-like shops were being readied for the day's business. Directly below the balcony, a man shoved a huge basket of melons through a door onto the pavement. The only traffic was a mule with a few sacks slung over his back. A man walked beside the mule, his head tilted up and turning from side to side, hawking whatever was in the bags, his mournful voice echoing down the wakening street.

There was a quaintness about the scene. Keeper might have watched it longer, but outside the odour of sulphur was more penetrating. Again he felt his throat tighten, his mouth dry up. As he stepped off the balcony, Holman entered the room carrying Keeper's suitcase.

'Thought you'd be about ready for this.'

Keeper took the valise and opened it on the bed. 'What stinks?'

'The springs,' Holman said. 'Hot springs.'

Everything in the suitcase seemed to be in order. Almost. A leather humidor that had held five cigars was empty, its top and bottom lying separately atop the folded clothes.

'That's what put Tbilisi on the map,' Holman went on. 'Fifteen hundred years ago a king was hunting near here. His falcon was chasing a pheasant, when suddenly it fell out of the air. The king searched for his bird and found it in a pool of water, boiled alive. So he built the capital of Georgia around the pool. "Tbili" is the Georgian word for "hot".'

Keeper grunted an appreciation of the anecdote as he buttoned his shirt. Standing by the window, Holman inhaled deeply. 'Why don't you try the springs, Keeper? Might do you good.'

'I didn't come here to be boiled alive.'

Holman laughed, then idly resumed his guidebook commentary on Tbilisi. Situated on the trade route between the Caspian and Black seas, it had long flourished as a stronghold of power, ruled successively by Arabs, Turks, and, finally, the Russians. It was also known as Tiflis.

As Holman rambled, Keeper heard two undertones: a genuine appreciation of Russian history, and a concern for relaxing his visitor. Recalling the way Holman had talked the night before about Susan, her need to rest from an ordeal, Keeper felt that the sympathy was real. Holman might be an ally.

They went down a broad marble staircase to a mirrored dining room and sat on gilt chairs at a long formal table while two men in white coats served ham and eggs (also in honour of the Americans?). The servers never raised their eyes, but concentrated on the plates, the table; they were obviously listening.

Keeper surveyed the elegant room. 'I thought they turned all the palaces into museums and apartment houses.'

'The Government maintains this one,' Holman explained, 'to accommodate visiting dignitaries.'

'I'm quite the dignitary,' Keeper observed, 'the father of a confessed enemy of the state.'

Holman shrugged. 'When Khrushchev came to New York he stayed at the Waldorf. At the same time he was trying to screw us in Germany, Cuba, you name it.'

'I guess that's what you call protocol,' Keeper said drily.

'Complaining? We're on the receiving end now.'

Keeper took the last bite of his ham and eggs and let the fork clatter onto the plate. 'I can't understand this new kind of world. We let the other side throw the rules out the window, then go right on drinking their champagne. Diplomats? You're pimps, Holman, you and your bosses. For the right price you fix up a circus between two diseased whores and let the whole world watch while they play with each other.'

Holman flushed. But his voice was carefully controlled:

'If diplomacy is a circus, then you just pray it stays in business. Because if it doesn't, then you'll see blood – casualties not just in the millions, but hundreds of millions.'

'Anything to avoid that,' Keeper said sourly. 'Even a total sellout, playing by their rules.'

Holman's chin jutted defiantly. Then, as he started to speak, the pose wilted. 'I'll admit it looks like a sellout. But we've been outmanoeuvred this time. It happens. Then whatever we do looks bad. But –' He stopped, his mouth open, the next word stillborn. One of the white-coated servants had come through a door at the end of the room carrying a silver coffeepot. He came to the table, filled the cups, and left the room.

'A great place to argue our policy,' muttered Holman. 'You realize the waiters are KGB?'

'Nice to know you care,' Keeper replied. 'I guess you'd rather talk while we're riding in our limousine, or helicopter – all provided by our considerate hosts.'

Holman picked up his coffee and sipped it intensely.

'While we're talking heart-to-heart,' Keeper went on, 'I get the feeling I've been shuttled down here to avoid upsetting somebody's apple cart. What do you know about it?'

Holman set his cup down very slowly. 'You're here for only one reason, Keeper. Because you asked to come. No, sorry, you don't ask, you don't have to. The country belongs to you. You just tell us what you want.' He paused. 'I'll tell you what I think. It's against my careful diplomatic training, but you deserve it. If you hadn't thrown your weight around, given someone at the other end a fat pain, you might have been saved this long useless trip.'

Keeper didn't mind hearing it. He would always trust the people who told him unflattering truths. Holman hadn't avoided an argument, nor smoothed over Keeper's accusations with pettifogging rhetoric. He'd stood up for his job. And yet he had defended its recent demands with the kind of snarling response that came of fighting in a corner. Perhaps Holman harboured his own honourable doubts about the manner in which things were being handled. Keeper wanted to test him further, but this was not the place.

They finished breakfast in silence. Leaving the table, Holman informed Keeper tersely that they would leave for Batumi as soon as Keeper was ready.

'That's too bad,' Keeper said. 'I thought we might get in some sightseeing.' Holman turned to him inquiringly. 'What the hell, I've got nothing else to do. You said I won't be able to see Roy until after the trial. That little travel talk of yours got me interested in this place.'

Holman shook his head. 'Are you serious?'

'Sure.'

They had left the dining room and were at the stairs.

'They won't like switching our travel plans,' Holman said.

'Not even for a "visiting dignitary"? Remind them we let Khrushchev see Disneyland.'

Holman smiled. 'I'll see what I can do. You get your stuff together.' He walked away across the vaulted entrance hall.

In his room, Keeper heard heated shouting rise from the downstairs hall. Collecting his suitcase quickly, he went down. It was the fat man shouting, the one who had taken his suitcase at the airport; he punctuated his tirade by poking a half-smoked cigar near to Holman's face.

Holman answered with constraint, his voice too low for Keeper to hear. Then he left the fat man and came over.

'They'll give us an extra thirty minutes.'

'Not much civic pride,' Keeper said. 'But I'll take what I can get. Pick out the most interesting spot in walking distance.'

Keeper had thought they would talk as they walked. But it was impossible, the noise in the street nearly deafening. Between the narrowly spaced buildings every inch was occupied by people, cars, and the wares piled in crude display outside the shops. Mules brayed and horns blared to clear a path through the colourful flood of movement. A mercenary chorus of vendors competed for business. One of them, a wizened cross-eyed man, stopped his mule as Keeper and Holman passed and leapt onto the sidewalk.

'Matsoni! Matsoni!' the vendor cried, pushing his face into Keeper's. Then just as quickly he was gone, accompanying his mule down the street.

'I look like his friend Matsoni,' Keeper yelled at Holman through the din.

'It's Georgian for "yoghurt",' Holman explained.

Keeper looked around at the ragged vendor and saw that he had been accosted by the fat man and a skinny companion, who were following the 'tour' at a distance of ten yards. They weren't buying any yoghurt.

Holman nudged Keeper ahead. 'It won't help the poor bastard if it looks like we care what happens to him.'

'What could they want with him?'

'They might have thought he was passing a message. They'll let him go.'

They walked on. Through several of the shop windows, Keeper saw pictures of Stalin tacked to the walls, some small, some huge life-sized posters.

'I thought he was taboo,' Keeper said.

'In this town, never. He's the local boy who made good.'

'He was born here?'

'Not in Tiflis, but in Georgia. Went to school here, though. The local seminary. If he hadn't been a dictator, he'd have been a priest.'

Where the enshrinement of Stalin had survived, Keeper thought, his methods might not have been renounced either. It wasn't the best part of the country for Roy to have to stand trial in.

Holman led the way down terraced slopes to the site he had chosen for the excursion. When they were standing enclosed by fragments of stone wall around a large central court, Holman said:

'These are the remains of the Anschiskat Basilica, built between the sixth and seventh centuries.' He pointed into a dark recessed niche. 'I could go on with a superb fifteen minutes on Byzantine art and religion, but I suspect you don't give a damn. You were too happy to settle for a lousy half hour. So I'll pretend to lecture while you do the talking.' He swung his arm to point in another direction at nothing in particular. Facing in the new direction, Keeper could check the present position of their fat and skinny shadows. They were maintaining a discreet distance. Keeper glanced away.

'Clever boy,' Keeper said. 'I have a feeling that maybe, like me, you're looking for answers. So I'm going to tell you a story, Holman. I've got to tell it fast and it may sound crazy, but make allowances.'

'I'm listening.'

As Keeper talked, Holman circled slowly around the vast stone floor of the basilica, maintaining the guise of calling attention to chiselled inscriptions, fragments of mosaic, checking constantly that the Russians were out of eavesdropping range.

In the telling, Keeper found it was not complicated, not unconvincing. The letter, Sealing's story, the visit to the hotel. Perhaps the passage of time and distance allowed him to put it together in a more compact, credible way; but Holman did not once turn a dumbfounded stare on Keeper as Fall had done. Or was it that Holman knew from experience how much might be done to achieve a political objective?

'Well, what do you think?' Keeper asked at the end.

Holman continued walking.

'What do you think?' Keeper repeated.

'I think you're out of your mind, coming all this way on a half-assed notion like that.'

'So you won't look into it?'

'Will it help you? It's easy enough for me to contact a pal in Moscow. If he peeps through the right keyhole, he'll see where the lady is supposed to be. But are you going to believe me when I come back and tell you? You might trust me, but can you trust my friend? And will you believe he looked through the right keyhole? Or that he saw the real Susan Keeper and not some made-up fake? You understand, Keeper? Once you get the kind of ideas you've got, the chain never ends.' Holman was looking hard at Keeper. Then, remembering the pose, he gestured instructively to the remains of the altar.

'Find one person who says he's actually seen her,' Keeper pressed, 'someone you trust, and I'll settle for that.'

The skinny Russian called something to Holman in a high-pitched reedy voice and pointed to his wristwatch.

'And one more thing,' Keeper said quickly. 'I'd like to know more about Yolkin. Anything you can dig up.'

The Russians were moving up behind them, prodding them out of the ruins. Holman gave no indication of what he would do about Keeper's requests.

'This should interest you,' he said loudly as they drifted towards the street. 'The Romans didn't build their first basilica for praying. It was a bank.'

Traveller's Russian

The helicopter flew a winding route of valleys, staying low except to clear an occasional snowcap. Then it would pass so close over the summit that small avalanches were chiselled loose by the jackhammer noise of the motor. Keeper watched them flake away from the white cones and slide in mute powdery clouds into skirts of vivid green like talcum cascading over the body of a plump young girl. The pilot also glanced down to watch the avalanches. He showed no alarm, no concern for lives endangered by the tons of falling snow; he knew the emptiness of the land. There were signs of life, but far from danger. Deep in a gorge, bisected by a gleaming ripple of water like the wavy blade of a kris, Keeper saw a couple of villages. And on some of the green plateaux herds of sheep were grazing. Once the pilot dropped his machine to skim over one of the herds, scattering the sheep in terror. A trio of barefooted shepherds ran after the helicopter, shaking their crooks while the pilot's face turned red laughing.

The landscape reminded Keeper of a part of Wyoming he had visited with Susan in the days before they were married. They had met in a military hospital in Nevada. After shipping home from the Pacific, Keeper had spent a month there recovering from a jungle fungus that was eating up his skin. She had been a nurse. The war was over, but not yet for so long that people were falling in love slowly again. As soon as Keeper was released from the hospital, she had taken him home to meet her parents.

They had hiked through the country she knew from her childhood. Had camped out and eaten food they hunted together. And at night, tired in the best way, not too tired to make love, they had rolled up in the same sleeping bag beside a fire to which they paced their touches, falling asleep by dying embers. It was a good memory, Keeper thought, the best he owned. It bothered him to know they might have gone on that way, stayed and lived on her territory, if he hadn't sacrificed it all to a dream. To be rich. They had gone back to his home in New Jersey, to the garage where the fortune began. Achieving the dream, finding it left him empty, Keeper wondered now if it had really been his own. Perhaps it was his father's dream, all the fathers, the nation's dream that, having fought to protect, he had unthinkingly adopted.

Little more than an hour after taking off, the helicopter leap-frogged the last mountain to the sea. The country they had flown over looked so wild that Keeper was surprised by the nearness of cities. But it was altitude and terrain that preserved the region's virginity, not vastness; it was a hard place to live.

They approached a coastal city. Keeper assumed it was Batumi. The pilot bypassed it, however, and flew out over the water for several minutes. Then he wheeled the helicopter in a wide circle so it came back above the coast several miles distant from the city. Keeper looked questioningly to Holman, who pointed down and shouted. His words were lost in the motor noise. It wasn't until after the pilot throttled back to float the helicopter over a large network of paths sectioning off a variety of flowers, shrubs and trees that Keeper understood. First, they had flown him out to the spot where Roy had been arrested. And below now were the Botanical Gardens where the aborted rendezvous was to have taken place. Their location, perched on a hill above the coast, suggested a sequence for Roy's plan. He would have landed in a small craft on the beach at the base of the hill; this could be left concealed in the lush foliage slightly inland of a narrow strand of beach. The forest-covered hillside would camouflage his climb up to the Gardens and return to the boat. Then he would be on his way, mission accomplished. Is this what they intended him to see now, that it might have been easily carried out? Keeper knew that lesson firsthand. During his own service in the Pacific he had been sent on a reconnaisance mission to a Japanese-occupied atoll. It hadn't been as death-defying as Hollywood commando raids had led him to expect. Under the right conditions, one could walk into enemy territory – at night, being ferried in close enough to shore so that the landing could be done quietly, swimming in, or paddling a raft.

Why, then, had Roy's rendezvous been planned for daylight, in a public place?

The question of the boat also rankled Keeper. Holman had told him Roy's claim to have used a rented fishing boat. The raft story had always seemed phony, so he had accepted Roy's version. But the crystalline water below showed shallow depths extending fairly far out from the beach. Only a small, flat-bottomed craft could have landed on this shore and been dragged into concealment; only something like a raft.

The helicopter luched forward, leaving the Gardens behind. Given what he had seen, Keeper tried to perceive a sensible plan designed to minimize risks. He could think of none. Apparently Roy had put himself in the hands of people unprepared to succeed in what they had attempted. Yet it was not entirely certain that they were amateurs.

They landed in a waterfront plaza, a square field of asphalt bordered by palm trees. As Keeper stepped out of the helicopter he saw uniformed men stationed between the trees, holding back curious onlookers. That was the full extent of any official reception.

The skinny man who had followed the morning's 'tour' had ridden along in the helicopter. He hunched ahead through the small tornado under the whirling rotor blades, one hand holding down his grey fedora, the other beckoning Keeper and Holman to follow. With Keeper carrying his suitcase, they walked towards a three-storey white building facing the sea at one end of the plaza, its curved protruding front stepped back like the bridge of a battleship.

The hotel's bare indecorous lobby looked like a hall that might be hired by crackpot political groups to hold sad, poorly attended meetings. An alcove at one side contained a registration desk. Part of the rear wall near a wide staircase had been crudely boarded up. Through wide spaces between the unpainted planks, Keeper saw a large area strewn with rubble. Broken tables and chairs lay partially buried under huge, jagged pieces of stone. An upside-down lake of sky showed through the collapsed ceiling.

'That was the dining room,' Holman said.

'Looks like a bomb hit it.'

'A building flaw. The hotel only opened last year. The contractor got twenty years.' Holman stepped away to the desk, where the skinny surveillance man was already having a heated exchange with the reception clerk, a large-boned but attractive girl with severely pulled back blonde hair. As Holman approached, the girl took a packet of letters from a rank of mailboxes and handed them over.

A short, bored-looking man with a flash camera entered the lobby and began taking pictures. At the first flash, the skinny man spun around tensely, but he turned back to the desk after a smile and a high sign from the photographer.

Then the conversation between the skinny man and the girl became angrier. As the girl moved patently closer to tears, Holman interceded. This only inflamed the thin man to new heights of ranting invective which Holman continued to answer in a level voice. Finally the thin man threw up his hands and Holman returned to Keeper grinning.

'I won that one.'

'What was the trouble?'

'Stringbean there didn't want you to carry your own luggage. There are no bellboys until after lunch – they're all in school now – so he told the clerk to do it. She wouldn't because she's the desk clerk, period; she'd rather die than take a step down the ladder.'

Keeper picked up the valise beside him. 'So what? I've been carrying –'

Holman grabbed the valise from Keeper. 'That was outside the hotel, now you're inside. Stringbean is determined to show us this place can match any Hilton. It's all part of the war.' He brought the suitcase to the desk and came back dangling a key. 'They'll send it up as soon as the bellboy comes on.'

'I thought you won.'

'I'm a diplomat. A compromise counts as a win. Especially around here.'

They were followed up the stairs by the photographer and the skinny man. Several times the dark stairwell was lit by the flash gun.

'What makes the back of my head so photogenic?' Keeper asked.

'He's snapping pictures for every newspaper and magazine in the world,' Holman replied. 'Whatever he takes, he'll sell. The Government has a permanent exclusive on all news pictures in Russia. You can imagine the dollars that brings in.' He chuckled. 'Leave it to the Russians – the last of the red-hot monopolists.'

'Do they write the stories for us, too?'

'No. We have correspondents.'

'Then, where are they?'

'Their movements are restricted. They need permits to travel down here, and nobody's got them yet.'

'So our side of the story won't be told.'

'Patience,' Holman muttered. 'They'll let one or two guys fly down to cover the trial.'

The photographer snapped a last burst of pictures as Keeper entered his room, but did not try to force his way in. After a short exchange with Holman, the skinny man also left.

'How do you like it?' Holman waved to the room.

'There are places I'd rather kill time.' It was plain and practical, the walls brightened only by three colour photographs that seemed to be snipped from travel magazines. Keeper sat down on the bed. He was sweaty and tired, but in a way that would keep him restlessly awake all day. His ears were still ringing from the helicopter motor.

'What do we do for amusement?'

Holman had started going through his mail. 'I'm afraid you're on your own, Keeper. Your son's bodyguard arrived while I was away. I have to meet with him.'

'Bodyguard? What for?'

'The Russians wanted one of their men to travel from the States with Yolkin. All conditions have to be equal.'

'Is protection routine?'

'Nothing's routine about these deals.'

Keeper paused. 'I want to know more about Yolkin, don't forget. I can't believe he's quite as ordinary as you say.'

'I can't oblige on that one, Keeper. I've told you all I know. Anything else would be hard to come by.'

'But there are ways. And it's worth trying. Whatever the Russians have done it's for Yolkin; he's the key. Now I want –'

'You want!' Holman broke in hotly. 'Look, I'll find out about the woman. But I'm not an errand boy to check on every little notion in your head.'

'And if you find out she's not around?' Keeper asked. 'Is that where you stop?'

Holman turned away, moving to the door. 'I'll be calling Moscow during the day. You'll have your answer tonight.'

Keeper didn't want Holman to go. Here, without the support of familiar surroundings, the prospect of solitude was suddenly unnerving. He spoke as much to delay Holman as to gain information, like a hospital patient subtly begging a few more seconds from a visitor.

'Will they let me move around on my own?'

'You can move around,' Holman said. 'You won't be alone.' He crossed quickly back to the window and motioned Keeper to stand beside him. Then he pointed into the street at a parked black sedan. 'One.' His finger shifted to a corner of the hotel; there, half-concealed in a side street, was another car. 'Two.' Then Holman nodded into the plaza at a man in shirtsleeves lounging against a palm tree. 'That's three. And Stringbean makes four.'

Keeper looked at the man by the tree. 'What gave him away?'

'You get to know the types,' Holman said. 'Some. There are undoubtedly a couple more I haven't spotted.' He drifted back to the door. 'But go where you want. They won't bother you unless you head off limits. A word to the wise,' he added. 'Don't try and lose them.'

'Why should I?'

'We're from a different world, Keeper. We're used to – at least an illusion of privacy. You think you won't mind these thugs? Wait 'til you start walking, and every time you turn around or tie your shoelace or look up from a drink there's one of them, staring right at you. Not hiding behind a newspaper or peeking out of a doorway, but right out in the open, his eyes riveted on you.' Holman laughed mirthlessly. 'You'll mind, brother. And they have a sixth sense. The itchier you get, the closer they'll follow. So you won't ditch them. If you try, you'll just confirm any suspicions they have. Which would make it harder on the rest of us.'

'I wouldn't want to do that,' Keeper said tartly.

Holman ignored it. 'There is a bright side. If you want a ride somewhere, hail one of those cars like a taxi. They'll take you where you want to go.'

'Any suggestions for my day off?'

'The Botanical Gardens is the number-one attraction in town.' Holman smiled thinly. 'But you've already seen that.'

There was a flash as he opened the door. The photographer was stationed outside.

'I'll pick you up for dinner,' Holman said and started away. Then he turned back. 'Oh, I bought something for you.' Patting his pockets, he came up with a booklet, which he flipped to Keeper before continuing down the corridor.

Traveller's Russian was the title on the cover. Keeper stood in the open doorway riffling through the English phrases with Russian translations given phonetically: YES. NO. GOOD MORNING. GOOD EVENING. CAN YOU RECOMMEND A GOOD RESTAURANT? IS THE TIP INCLUDED? DO YOU HAVE A ROOM WITH DOUBLE BED? The predictable dole of tourist prattle. But he was another kind of traveller. Where was the phrasebook for him? CAN YOU RECOMMEND SOMEONE TO TRUST? I AM LOOKING FOR A WOMAN. SHE IS DEAD? SHE IS ALIVE? MY SON IS A SPY, A FOOL . . . ?

He had decided to rest until his bag was sent up. A shave and change of clothes and he could make the best of a walk through the town, or along the sea. But the confinement was stifling. Keeper felt as though he was suffocating in the hot wet air. He went to the window and opened it. A dank, uncooling breeze came off the ocean.

The helicopter, the uniformed men and the sprinkling of onlookers had gone from the plaza. It was empty except for the swarthy man in shirtsleeves Holman had pointed out. He was still propped against the same palm tree. Reflected rays from the high sun bounced off the low whitewashed buildings around the plaza, stealing the shade from under the floppy palm fronds, depriving the watcher of camouflage. But he was not concerned with hiding. His eyes burned directly at Keeper's window. Like lasers, they seemed to transmit some heat of their own, making the room closer, more unbearable.

Keeper was about to go when there was a knock on the door. A scrawny teen-aged boy stood outside, holding the suitcase. He brought it into the room and set it down. Keeper held out a handful of coins; he had no Russian money, but the boy would no doubt value an American coin even more.

The boy refused the tip with a solemn shake of his head. Taking something from his own pocket, he dropped it into Keeper's outstretched palm. Then, with an oddly oriental bow, he let himself out of the room.

Keeper looked into his hand. Among the coins, wadded so tightly it was almost lost under them, was a bit of paper, like an old spitball from the child's pocket. Keeper tried to open it. As though removing the shell of a tiny hard nut, he had to pry at the spitball with his fingernail to start peeling away the edge. Whoever had compressed the paper had more than the strength of a child, more than an ordinary man.

The paper was of a wafery translucent quality. Fully open, with the wrinkles smoothed out, it proved to be a fairly large diagrammatic map of interconnecting streets, with several landmarks identified in English at turning points: 'statue of Stalin'; 'stone fountain with fish'; 'seller of carpets'. Arrows traced a route through the streets, starting at the hotel and finishing at a box under which was written 'house with black shutters'. There was a note at the bottom.

COME PLEASE. WE ARE FRIENDS TO YOUR SON. TRY TO BE NOT FOLLOWED.

It was unsigned.

A number of careless features struck Keeper about the note. The last cautionary sentence of the message which used the word 'try' – as if failing to elude surveillance should not deter him from keeping the implied appointment. And the diagram: it was simple enough that it might have been crammed onto a much smaller piece of paper, which Keeper could have referred to as he made his way without attracting undue attention. Oversized as it was, he couldn't refer to it en route without being conspicuous. Neither the note nor the map had been conceived by a mind intent on secrecy.

Scrutinizing the pencilled lines, Keeper wondered if they had been drawn by hand. Minute angular squiggles along their length indicated the work of something mechanical, some sort of vibrating stylus. At one place in the diagram an erratic motion had seemingly forced the stylus down, tearing the paper. A patch of identical paper had been glued over the torn spot, and the interrupted pencil lines retraced.

He folded the map accordion-fashion, small enough to fit into his hand, then put it in his pocket. It would be safer to use this way, if he used it at all. Even assuming some good could come of a visit to the house with black shutters, there was a big obstacle to be cleared first. Four obstacles, for that matter, maybe more. Keeper craned towards the window, trying to see without being seen. The man by the palm tree stared up at the room, unblinking, his stance unchanged.

Vultures. His only hope of eluding them was to do it right at the start, leave the hotel undetected. The disadvantage would be too great afterwards. He didn't know the city; they did. It wasn't enough to outrun them; he could break away only to turn into a cul-de-sac, or be headed off via some short cut.

His resentment at being watched, the feeling Holman had warned against, tripped the balance. Nobody could pen him up this way.

In his moment of resolve, Keeper had the door already open when he remembered the photographer. But there was no flash. The corridor outside was empty. Evidently they had expected him to stay in his room.

Or had the escape been deliberately simplified, made more tempting?

Keeper tiptoed into the corridor, closed the door softly behind him. A voice singing plaintively to the accompaniment of a balalaika wafted faintly along the passage, getting louder as Keeper came to the stairway. A radio, he thought, from the lobby just below. He didn't take the stairs, but searched the two wings on either side looking for a way out. Gingerly turning the knobs on all the doors, exerting a slight pressure, he found every one locked. Breaking one open would be too noisy.

The main stairs were the only way down.

He met no one as he descended.

In the lobby, the boy sat alone in one of the plain chairs lining one wall, pensively picking his nose. The balalaika song filtered out through a closed door behind the registration counter. Beneath its strains, Keeper heard a man's seductive murmuring, a girl's not very determined rebuffs, intermittent giggling.

So that was where the photographer had gone. But they were an unlikely pair of lovebirds – the young, attractively intense desk clerk and the bored, toad-faced photographer. And it was the girl, Keeper recalled, who had insisted on waiting for the boy to carry the luggage. Part of the plan?

As Keeper hesitated on the bottom step, the boy saw him. He rose from the chair and walked to the gerry-built wall of boards; he showed hardly any change from the adolescent apathy displayed while picking his nose, didn't seem particularly thrilled or frightened to participate in this intrigue. The gesture he made for Keeper to join him was languid, almost nonchalant.

The boy pulled four long nails smoothly from their holes in one of the planks, freeing it to swing aside. This left a gap in the wall wide enough for Keeper to step through. He paused in front of the space; it was all too damn easy.

The boy squealed suddenly: 'Poshlee!' and again more urgently when Keeper was slow to respond. 'Poshlee! Poshlee!' The burst of panic, proof that there were risks, propelled Keeper through the gap. On the other side of the wall he stopped to look back. The board had already been replaced; through a crack, Keeper saw the boy strolling to his chair.

He scanned the roofless room. At the far end were double doors. Holman had said this was the dining room; the doors probably led to a kitchen. Beyond that there would be a service access, a way out. He tried to make his way soundlessly over the rubble, but the chunks of fallen ceiling that covered the floor teetered on their jagged edges. Every step produced a gritty scraping, an echoing clatter. Then as he reached the middle of the room, he heard an extra noise somewhere behind him. He stopped. Again from the rear came a rasp of shifting stones. Turning abruptly, he saw a large yellowish rat scurry between two shards of concrete.

He took a breath. Now he noticed the windows staring down through the yawning hole above. Perhaps he was being watched from up there, every step of his escape studied as though he were a rat in a maze. Still, he couldn't turn back. He dodged under the broken knuckles of ceiling that clung to the top of a wall, and ran through the double doors.

The mammoth kitchen, tiled in green ceramic, was immaculate. The only evidence of any use was a loaf of bread sitting on the corner of a butcher's block, a long-bladed knife lying beside it. Keeper stopped to touch the knife. Would he need something for protection? He decided against the weapon and moved on to a narrow pantry lined with iceboxes. This terminated at another door, a slab of metal secured by an iron bolt. He teased the bolt aside, inched the door open. A sliver of daylight widened to a view of the back alley, a long empty stretch of pavement. Referring to the diagram, he saw that 'behind of hotel' had been written next to the first arrow. It pointed away from a junction with the side street in which Holman had spotted a surveillance car. At the other end of the alley the arrows turned a corner at a grid marked 'stair – some loose careful'. For amateurs, Keeper thought, they hadn't done a bad job of providing a fast trouble-free escape. If anything, they had done too well.

He looked back at the knife gleaming on the chopping block, hesitated, then stepped out into the day.

Bookworm

The map led him through a section of new buildings, square and squat as though stamped out by some titanic cookie cutter. Here the streets were crowded; he could not be sure that no one was following. Whenever he glanced back, Keeper saw the same nondescript collection of shoppers and strollers: older women carrying shopping bags, wearing drab shapeless coats too warm for the weather; younger women, looking younger only because they wore no coats; grim grey men of indeterminate age.

As the city began climbing the side of a hill the new section ended, streets narrowed to sloping walkways cobbled with immense white stones worn smooth by centuries of scuffing feet. The crowd thinned and disappeared, and Keeper could see no one trailing him. Yet he did not feel alone. Behind the walls that bordered his route there was hectic activity. He heard the incessant coughing of a saw cutting through a piece of wood, the sparking ring of metal on metal. Smells of leather, fruit, baking bread, sweat and machine oil stole out of doorways. But they were reluctant leaks. This was a neighbourhood that did not welcome strangers. The windows of shops gave no more than a hint of the nature of their business, signposts for friends: a single tin can, a shoe, an axe.

Farther on, the walkways became mere dirt channels running ragged up the hillside. And there, standing apart from a cluster of small huts, Keeper saw the house, the only one that had two floors. For a moment, though he had meticulously followed the map, he wondered if he had taken a wrong turn somewhere. The shutters of the house were not black, but a thundercloud grey. Then he realized they had once been black, long ago; their present colour was one in a rainbow of neglect. The mottled ochre of stucco walls, crumbling like stale cake; the brown of a rusty rain gutter sagging from the eaves. Overgrown bushes and vines wrestled for space in the surrounding yard.

Where a gate would have stood if the fence had not rotted and collapsed, Keeper took one more long look behind him. Fifty yards of barren scrub ground separated him from the end of the nearest cobbled street. An old woman, her back extremely bowed, was picking her way crablike down the hill. There was nobody else in sight. Standing here, Keeper felt dangerously exposed. There were a hundred corners from which secret eyes might be watching. The choice of this meeting place had been stupid. Why not a back room, a cellar? Anywhere was better than a large house standing apart on the side of a hill.

A path led to a platform of stone steps up to the entrance. As he reached the top step the door, a solid oak panel with a split running from top to bottom, swung open. Framed in the doorway was a small pretty girl, about twenty years old. She had dark sad eyes and short scraggly chestnut hair that looked as though it had been cut by her own hands without the aid of a mirror. Her clothes, a threadbare brown skirt and heavy black sweater riddled with moth holes, underlined her melancholy aspect.

She motioned Keeper inside with a single nervous flick of her hand, then shut the door so quickly as he entered that he had not yet moved clear; the edge of the door banged his elbow. The accident pained the girl more than Keeper. She touched his arm and murmured something forlornly apologetic. A sudden film of tears glistened in her dark eyes.

'It's all right,' Keeper said. The depth of her concern reassured him that he was not walking into a trap. The girl was rigid with shame, hungering for another word from him. 'Really. It's fine,' he said.

She smiled then and led him to a stairway. As they climbed, Keeper saw into a few rooms leading off the central foyer. Sunlight squeezing through the closed shutters striped their bare wooden floors. The rooms were all empty of furniture.

More unfurnished rooms lined the second-floor corridor. But these seemed to be in use. Cutouts from magazines and pencil sketches were taped to the walls. And piles of blankets were spaced around the floors, evenly as in a dormitory. At the end of the hall the girl stopped by a door and pointed in. Then she walked away and down the stairs.

Inside the small room dark towers loomed up to the ceiling, silhouetted by a glow from somewhere beyond. As Keeper advanced, he saw that the towers were stacks of books arranged in aisles, each stack standing alone, precariously unbolstered.

'Be very careful,' said a man's voice. 'They will fall at a touch. Then we would really see the domino theory in action.' Keeper went towards the speaker, who was still hidden. 'Forgive the darkness,' the voice added, 'but bright light is painful to my eyes.'

Walking gingerly between the stacked books, Keeper saw titles in several languages: French, Italian, German, English and Greek. *The Rise and Fall of the Third Reich* was one in English; *Soul on Ice*, another. There were also some James Bond thrillers. The German books were thick with long titles, probably texts. Many of the French titles included the names of painters.

He emerged into an arena of light cast by a kerosene lantern set on a wooden crate. Now Keeper saw his host. He was in a bed, end on to a wall, his back supported by a sling that had been secured to the wall by thick ropes. A separate harness for his head was rigged to wires suspended from the ceiling. All the ropes and wires were fed through pulleys, then linked up to two paramount ropes that dangled straight down, the ends hanging just above the hands that lay limply on the blankets. He was at once a puppet and his own puppeteer. Yet somehow, even imprisoned in this contraption, he was not pathetic. The strength that had gone out of his wasted torso had seemingly flowed upward into the part of his body that showed above the sheets. His head and shoulders were those of a Cossack centaur, long black hair, eyes like black onyx marbles, the tendons of his neck thick as bridge cables.

He rolled his head towards Keeper. 'Thank you for coming, Mr Keeper. I am Kiril Culdiev.'

Keeper studied the interlacing of wires and ropes. He understood now why the map had been drawn shakily, outsized. Making it at all had been a considerable feat.

'What was it,' Keeper asked bluntly, 'an accident?'

Culdiev replied easily; he appreciated the frankness. 'Disintegration of nerve matter, they tell me. A reasonable excuse, I suppose, for the fact that only a small fraction of me still takes orders from my brain. But there are curious side effects to the disease that make me question the diagnosis. For instance, the more this nerve matter disintegrates, the nervier I get.'

'Like sending me that note . . .'

'That was only a small risk,' Culdiev said.

'What if I'd been followed?' Pointedly, Keeper added, 'Although the note indicated you weren't overly worried whether or not I was.'

'Ah!' Culdiev smiled. 'I did not stress the importance of eluding the K G B, so as not to frighten you from coming. But of course it would be bad if you were followed. So all along the way you were watched by friendly angels who made sure you were not watched by the Devil. If there had been danger you would have been warned off long before reaching this house.'

'That's another thing,' Keeper said, 'this house. There must be safer places to meet.'

'Many,' Culdiev agreed. 'Shall we go for a walk, you and I, to find one?'

Keeper said nothing.

Culdiev, sounding apologetic as if ashamed of having used his infirmity to make a point, went on. 'Never mind, Mr Keeper, we are safe enough here. In this house twenty years ago there lived a family who fell into a blood feud. The details do not weigh, except that in the end one of the three daughters was hacked to death with a sabre.' Culdiev chuckled. 'In this wonderful country of progress and pragmatism, all superstition has not been eliminated. A house that has seen such a feud is considered evil, cursed. It is left vacant and shunned, even by people who like to consider themselves enlightened. So for those who are brave and poor it makes a good place to live. And not a bad place to meet those who are brave and rich.'

It was not flattery, Keeper thought, the attribution of courage. Before the meeting was over, Culdiev would dare him to deserve the compliment. 'Who are you, Culdiev? What do you want?'

Without lifting his hand, the Russian swivelled the index finger to point at the room's source of light, the lantern on the crate. 'Move that to the floor, please, you will have a seat. At this stage of my life it demoralizes to see anyone stand for too long.'

When Keeper had moved the lantern and sat down, Culdiev said, 'I ask you here to receive apology, sir. I am to blame for troubles of your son.'

'You? You're the boss of the samizdat network?'

'Boss? Is what?'

'The head, the leader.'

Culdiev closed his eyes a moment, committing the slang to memory. Then he said, 'I think then I am not boss.'

'But you're responsible for bringing in Roy.'

'Ah, yes,' Culdiev sighed. 'Responsible.' The onyx marbles glinted at Keeper, appraising him for another moment. Then Culdiev turned away to look straight at the wall. His jaw set firmly as though in preparation for an ordeal. And now it began. He lifted his arms from the blanket so slowly, so agonizingly, that, merely in watching, Keeper's muscles tightened sympathetically. Reaching for the ends of rope suspended from above, Culdiev's hands rose one scant millimetre at a time. Pain disfigured the young Russian's handsome face, made even more grotesque by the lantern light thrown up from the floor. It was a full minute before Culdiev had elevated his hands the few inches to grab the ropes. Pulling them down, which took even longer and was evidently more painful, positioned the sling so that he was finally sitting up, looking directly at Keeper.

As though there had been no more than a momentary break in the conversation, Culdiev resumed. 'I must go back a little to explain this responsibility. Five years ago I was a student. I had friends who wrote stories and poems. Sometimes they produced work that our teachers disapproved; pieces which contained certain sentiments, you understand. But if I knew these were good, I would pass them around. It was not a crusade; at first there was no danger. But then the mood changed. The

111

censors became more hard. Writers we had respected were being sent to prison. And then students. Also, it was at that time I found out ...' He paused, eyes down, for one second a mourner at his own funeral. 'I didn't mind then to take chances. I had nothing to fear. So I was put at the centre of people in this region who cared about free expressing of ideas. I became like a' – he groped for the right word, indistinctly mumbling and rejecting a few – 'a switchboard.' He grinned, triumphantly proud of his English. 'This was still not a daring thing. I knew where certain books could be found, I would tell those who wished to know. I had names of people who would make copies. All in my head. But we were not copying work of famous writers, those you know in the West, simply of men who had written well and were denied their chance to be read. It was, as you say, a two-bits operation.'

'It took guts,' Keeper said. 'I wouldn't price it so low.'

Culdiev acknowledged the praise with a thin smile. 'I was not so satisfied. I saw my death coming. Before the end I wanted to do something more, to make a difference.' He paused. 'Do you care about books, Mr Keeper?'

'I never had much time for them,' Keeper replied.

Culdiev nodded. 'Look at me, sir. Can you imagine how I love them? In books I can leave this bed, ride white stallions, run through forests, sail the ocean. And when I am in bed it is not as this rotten fragment of a man, but whole, able to take a woman and fuck her.' He fell silent; his eyes were distant, as if watching his passion fly away like a lost kite.

'You see the meaning of books to a cripple,' he continued finally. 'And we are so many cripples here, unable to do or say so much we would like. I knew *The Mushroom Cave* would help. By weakening our enemies it would make us stronger. So I had to try ...' His eyes searched Keeper's. Begging, Keeper thought; for approval, or forgiveness.

Keeper leaned over the bed. It smelled clean, fresh, without the odour of sickness. 'Then you've got Lyndushkin's book?'

Culdiev hesitated. 'No,' he said tonelessly. 'I never saw it.'

'But you sent for Roy.'

'Yes, it was a chance ...' His voice faded, his shoulders were trembling.

'Jesus,' Keeper whispered. He sat back on the crate. Questions streaked through the dark of his mind like comets, faint, nebulous but phenomenal. Was there a book? Or was it only a legend Lyndushkin's jailers had unwittingly fostered by acting on their fear?

The Russian was straining forward. 'I see now I decided badly. But I haven't much more life. This was the opportunity . . .' Culdiev sank into the sling again; the pulsing veins in his neck subsided into the flesh. 'Let me explain how it came to me. Three months ago a student named Folscha found his way here. He said he knew of a manuscript of *The Mushroom Cave* and begged me to arrange for getting it West before it was destroyed. I knew people with the necessary contacts, but I was wary of Folscha. He had turned up too suddenly. So I refused.'

'And then changed your mind.'

'Folscha came back again and again. His fear that the manuscript would be lost began to impress me.'

'Why didn't you ever ask to see the manuscript?'

'I did, repeatedly. But Folscha said it would best remain where Lyndushkin had hidden it until it could be taken out of the country. I could not object to this caution. Even before Lyndushkin died there were rumours he had written this book long ago *dlya yaschika*, as we say: for the drawer; to be kept hidden until the author is beyond punishment. Since his death there have been more whispers – copies of the book found, only to be seized and immediately destroyed. Now it has become for us . . . like a Grail.'

'Worth any gamble,' Keeper put in, 'no matter who gets hurt.'

Culdiev hesitated. 'If you must put it that way, yes. So I sent word through my contacts to the same man who helped bring *The Orchestra* to the West, a publisher in Paris. I received a message in return. Someone would come for the book. A date was given, a meeting place was specified –'

'The Gardens?' Keeper asked.

'Yes. All this Folscha agreed. But with some adjustments. He would not divulge the hiding place, or allow it to be taken from there by any but the man who would bring it West. He wanted to meet the agent at the Gardens and lead him to the hiding place. The manuscript would then be given and the agent left to make – what is it? – a getaway.'

How well, Keeper wondered, did Culdiev comprehend the long reach of decisions made while imprisoned in his bed. Perhaps he was only relieving the tedium of his invalid life with an egghead version of cops and robbers, imitating the same thrillers that had taught him his slang.

'I've seen the Gardens,' Keeper said. 'Seems like a good place to make the transfer, near the water. Folscha's plan would only have increased the risks.'

'For the agent, yes. But it would be much safer for our man at the Gardens not to wait with the manuscript in hand. Like Folscha, I thought the greatest risk should be taken by the man with training, someone whose profession is to –'

Keeper broke in excitedly. 'You were told that the man coming for the book was a professional, a trained agent?'

'As I say, it was one reason to agree with Folscha.'

'And the others?'

'Simply that I had no choice. The messages about this could not be sent quickly. I would talk to someone, he would pass my word to another – I don't know who – a sympathetic official with rights to travel, perhaps, or a sailor on merchant ship going through the port. A single contact might take four, five, six weeks. By the time I received my answer from Paris only two weeks remained to the rendezvous date. There was no way to call off the plan, or get approval of Folscha's new conditions. So we proceeded.' He paused. 'With one more adjustment. On the day of the meeting, Folscha did not go to the Gardens. Another was sent; Anastas, a nice boy, very dedicated . . .' Culdiev frowned, a paternal look of concern misplaced on his young face.

'Why didn't Folscha go?'

Culdiev shrugged. 'He wanted to stay at the hiding place, be with the book in case anything went wrong.'

'Then he had to tell where the agent should be brought.'

'Folscha revealed the hiding place to Anastas immediately before he went to the Gardens. As Anastas was arrested there, and Folscha disappeared the same day, I never learned . . .'

Keeper perceived new outer limits to the plan the Russians

had laid for bringing Yolkin home. 'There was no hiding place, Culdiev, nothing to learn. Folscha was planted on you.'

'His disappearance proves nothing,' Culdiev answered sharply. 'Yes, he might be K G B, part of some plan to use us. But also he could have been frightened into hiding by what happened to Anastas.' He rotated stiffly to look more fully at Keeper. 'This is why I take chance to talk with you. If we are being used, I must know, so I can close down the network; if not, our work can go on. You can give the answer, perhaps. Tomorrow the trial begins. No Russians will be allowed to attend except officials. But you will be there. If Folscha appeared to testify against Anastas, or evidence were submitted that could only come from him –'

'I could tell you about it,' Keeper filled in, 'give you a full report of what happens at the trial.'

Culdiev's black eyes held steady on Keeper.

'Forget it,' Keeper said.

'We can minimize the risk, sir,' Culdiev pleaded. 'You have but to write down the information. Your messages can be brought from the hotel.'

'No dice,' Keeper muttered, a consolation prize of slang for Culdiev's collection.

Culdiev, unable to move his arms, to reach out and appeal to Keeper, pitched in his sling. 'Mr Keeper, please. You cannot deny us this help!'

'Why not?' Keeper said harshly. 'Out of pity for you? How do I really know which side you're on? You could be rigged out like this just to prey on my sympathy, lure me on ...'

Culdiev's eyes shone hard and cold like black ice. Out of silence rose a chittering squeak, the laughter of mice, rising from hilarity to hysteria before Keeper realized it came from the bedsprings, shaking under the constrained fury of Culdiev's body.

Slowly one hunchbacked hand crawled across the blanket, clutched at one corner and tried to fling it back. But disease strangled the panache. The sick fingers could only claw away the blanket, then the sheet beneath, inch by inch, as though removing the rind of a tough white fruit. Finally the legs were unveiled, protruding from his nightshirt, gnarled and shrunken

115

bones encased loosely in mottled barklike skin. They lay flopped over one another, discarded remnants, punctuated at the end of each foot by blackened toenails. A wave of nausea swelled within Keeper, disgust with what he saw, and with himself.

'Do not be ashamed,' Culdiev said at last. 'You were right to make sure.' He struggled to cover himself again.

Keeper quickly pulled up the sheet. He wanted to leave now, but felt bound by his shame to stay; he owed Culdiev something.

'Never mind what I hear at the trial,' he said. 'I'll tell you right now enough to tip the balance against Folscha.'

'Against – ?'

'After the trial my son will be traded for a Russian spy being held by my government. It's all arranged.'

Culdiev made a short humming sound. 'But these exchanges have been done before. What does it mean about Folscha?'

'You said he came to you three months ago. It was around that time the man who's being sent back here was arrested.'

Culdiev thought, then said adamantly, 'I think you are misled by coincidence.'

'I'll tell you a little more; then decide who's been misled. First, my son isn't a trained agent. Second, it seems he was set up to be taken at sea, without ever landing. That leaves your Anastas waiting for a rendezvous that was never going to take place.'

'This does not make sense,' Culdiev protested. 'If K G B made a trap they would better to have caught your son here.'

'Possibly. But whoever they suckered in would agree quicker to a plan which didn't include a landing, just an outing in an old boat. The Russians have turned that into a pretty good case as it is.'

'No,' Culdiev pouted, 'I do not believe.'

Keeper studied Culdiev. The maturity that had seemed so much a part of him had vanished; he had turned into a stubborn child, refusing to listen or take part in debate. Having asked for information, he should have been drawing Keeper out. Instead, he had abruptly closed off discussion.

Keeper glanced away, exasperated, on the verge of going. But then, seeing the dark towers of books, he understood. They were the totems of Culdiev's religion. Like any true believer, Culdiev could only go through the motions of doubt, backing off the moment his doubts began to assume substance. It wasn't knowing whether or not Folscha was KGB that really mattered; it was knowing whether or not Lyndushkin's precious Grail was real.

'You'd really like to hear it one way, wouldn't you, Culdiev? Not to prove Folscha guilty, but innocent. So you can believe the book exists.'

'Of course it exists,' Culdiev said sullenly. 'Whatever is true of Folscha, you cannot say there is no book. The stake is whether it is here in Batumi.'

'You've only heard of it in rumours,' Keeper persisted. 'Maybe that's all there ever was.'

'No!' Culdiev's head reared back. The wires of the harness sang in the pulleys. 'He would not let the truth be buried.'

'Lyndushkin?' Keeper jeered. 'How did he earn such reverence as a prophet of truth? If he did write about the purge, how did he come by the story? By being part of it, one of the butchers.' Pain was showing through Culdiev's mask of defiance, but Keeper didn't let up. 'And suppose the book is found. Couldn't it be lies, Lyndushkin's way of getting even with the men who would have chopped him if he hadn't skipped out thirty years ago?'

' "Skipped out"?' Culdiev looked puzzled.

'Ran for his life. Disappeared.'

The cloud of resistance around Culdiev evaporated. 'Now I see why you have doubted. There has been some mystery about how Lyndushkin survived the purge. But among those who talk of such things, the story has come piece by piece. True, he was with secret police, and when the purges began he was raised in position. Only then, as he gained importance, did he learn fully what was happening, the madness. It sickened him. But he could not find a way to . . . skip out.

'He was found in his office one day unable to speak except to make strange beast noises. There was blood coming from his ears. He had suffered a stroke, it was plain. Much of his body was paralysed. They put him in a hospital and watched him closely. For four years he was there, never talking. At last they

117

released him. He began to walk a little; but not for thirty years that anyone knows did he ever talk. Then Khrushchev came up and things were loose; and miraculously at this time Lyndushkin recovered. Only his hearing remained slightly impaired. That, you see, was the only loss that was real. When he pushed the nails into his ears to make them bleed, he had punctured both eardrums.'

Culdiev's eyes were moist. One of his hands twitched, as if he wanted to lift it and wipe his eyes. But the effort was too great.

Keeper thought Culdiev's belief in the story more touching than the story itself; that was only another part of the myth.

'Before and during the last war,' Culdiev went on, 'while Lyndushkin was still an "invalid", he lived near here. There are hot springs in the region. He came for their curative effect, to keep up the pretence. The house he occupied has been torn down, where they have built some new city. But it is logical to believe the book is here. So you accept now?'

'No,' Keeper said. 'I don't accept that Lyndushkin's a saint simply because he managed to save his own sweet skin.'

Culdiev's cheeks grew more orange in the golden light coming from the lantern. 'You have heard of Pasternak? Of course. A hero, a martyr in the struggle to free our minds. But there is this story. Once Stalin telephoned Pasternak. Stalin had been told that a poet named Osip Mandelstam had written a violently hateful poem against him and was reading it to gatherings of intellectuals. So he called Pasternak to ask if this was true. And what did Pasternak answer? He said only that he didn't know the man very well. So Mandelstam went to a prison camp, where he lost his mind and starved to death.'

Keeper waited a moment. 'And what's the moral?'

'The moral is that there is no moral. If Pasternak had lied he could have saved a good man; he said a fact, the man died. So the truth itself may be a fly-specked thing, given from hands that are slightly soiled. But we are beggars for truth here, Mr Keeper, we go hungrily for scraps.'

There was, after all, a kinship of interests, Keeper reflected. He was also a beggar for truths withheld. Though he still thought Culdiev nurtured an illusion, Keeper decided to help him plod towards that realization in his own good time – what was left of it.

'All right, Culdiev. If I hear something at the trial that would interest you, I'll pass it along.'

As if she had been waiting for Culdiev to win, to play his final scene, the girl materialized suddenly from the shadowland of books. In one hand she held a glass of water, in the other a number of pills. She placed the tablets on Culdiev's tongue and decanted the water gently into his mouth. Then she stepped to the foot of the bed and stood there against the wall like a sentry, a loving sentry. She exchanged a tender smile with Culdiev, and Keeper saw a dream smoulder in the Cossack eyes.

'She is the only one who stayed with me after Folscha disappeared,' Culdiev said. There was a long pause, heavy with threadbare hopes, then he turned from the girl to Keeper. 'One of the pills was for sleeping. In fifteen minutes I will doze away. Before I would like to read a little. Would you think me rude – ?'

Keeper rose from the crate. 'I was just going.'

'Shake my hand, please. An American good-bye.'

Keeper picked up Culdiev's hand and gripped it. The response was slow and weak, as though the brain's command travelled across light years to the cold fingers. But it had begun as an intense flash; the feeling was strong, if unseen. As Keeper let go, the girl went to a stack of books taller than herself and reached down the top volume. Cracking it open at a marker, she laid the book in Culdiev's lap and arranged his arms to serve as a bookstand. Then she led Keeper out.

He was halfway down the hall when he heard Culdiev begin to read aloud:

' "So I made Jim lay down in the canoe and cover up with a quilt 'cause if he set up people could tell he was a nigger from a long way off. I paddled over to the Illinois shore ..." '

Keeper knew the book, one of the few he would never forget reading. Mouthing its dialect, Culdiev's accent sounded comically thick, ridiculous.

As the girl opened the front door, Keeper paused and listened to a little more, faintly audible from upstairs.

' "After breakfast I wanted to talk about the dead man and

guess out how he come to be killed, but Jim didn't want to. He said it would fetch bad luck; and besides, he said, he might come and ha'nt us; he said a man that warn't buried was more likely to go a-ha'nting around than one that was planted and comfortable. That sounded pretty reasonable, so I didn't say no more; but I couldn't keep from studying over it and wishing I knowed who shot the man and what they done it for . . ." '

Going down the hill, Keeper started laughing. A Russian Huck Finn. That was a hot one.

Confirmation

The boy was still sitting in an empty lobby picking his nose. A tap on the planking brought him running to yank out the loose nails and slide away the board.

Upstairs, the corridor was empty, the photographer had not taken up his post again.

And from the terrace outside his room when Keeper looked into the plaza, he saw the same man leaning against the palm tree, his face tilted up at the room, silvered with perspiration. Nothing had changed; no one had missed him.

Surely they knew, had wanted to make the escape easy, let him think his absence went unnoticed. But if Folscha was KGB, there would be a watch on Culdiev's house, they would have seen Keeper visiting. Wanting to keep Folscha in the clear, however, they would not reveal themselves.

A sudden awareness of hunger and fatigue pushed the speculation out of his mind. He needed food, needed to sleep; his bones felt hollow, his stomach clenched and small. He went to the bed and sat on it, considered what to do about getting a meal. But before he could decide, he sank back onto the bed, asleep.

When he woke, the room was dim in the purple light of evening. Someone was knocking on the door, softly but with a quick urgent tempo.

'Keeper?' It sounded like Holman.

Keeper hauled himself off the bed, swayed blearily to the door and opened it. Food was the first thing on his mind.

'Suppertime?'

'Yeah, I'm starving. C'mon.' Something in Holman's tone said that food was the last thing on his mind.

While Keeper splashed cold water on his face, Holman stalked the room impatiently.

121

'You ready yet?' he asked when Keeper was combing his hair.

'Where's the fire?'

'Sorry.' Holman moved into the doorway of the bathroom. 'Am I bugging you?'

The question sounded out-of-key until Keeper saw Holman in the mirror, pantomiming the message – one hand cupped over his ear, the other waving around at the walls.

Nothing more was said until they were outside the hotel, crossing the asphalt square to the sea wall at its far end.

Then Holman said, 'Walk slower. We're out for a casual evening stroll.'

As they passed one of the palm trees, Keeper saw the shadow of a man straighten from a leaning position, preparing to fall in behind them.

They came to the wide promenade that ran along by the sea wall. Lining its inland side was a long row of ramshackle cafés, narrow open stalls. From each enclosure came the weak glow of one or two moth-encrusted bulbs, back-lighting for a chain of huddled silhouettes, men grouped around flimsy metal tables on the sidewalk. Their conversation merged to a low murmured babble, uncommonly subdued for café habitués.

Holman chose to walk on the opposite side of the promenade, beside the sea wall. Tonight the sea was unruly. High waves rolled into the stone barrier with loud swashing crashes, spattering small showers up onto the promenade. Keeper didn't mind the water; it was warm. Holman had sought the noise, he realized, to drown out their words.

Holman paused to light a cigarette. The first two matches were doused by spray. Turning his back on the sea, he finally saved a flame – and checked the distance at which they were being followed. Then they walked on.

'It's probably not worth all this trouble,' Holman said. 'What I'm going to tell you came over the phone, so the odds are they already picked it up. But we don't do any serious talking in hotel rooms; that's a rule.'

Keeper anticipated Holman's business. 'Is she there?'

'No.'

Keeper stopped and stared at Holman. Gripping his arm, Holman pulled him ahead.

'Are you positive?' Keeper said quickly.

'Absolutely.'

'Then what the hell –'

'I don't know, Keeper, I don't know. But as it turns out, that's beside the point.'

'Beside the point?' Keeper echoed heatedly.

A big wave whomped into the wall, spraying them with droplets. Holman was oblivious, concentrating on what he had to say. 'Remember I had an appointment this morning with the man who's going to chaperone Roy. I was supposed to fill him in on the situation here: general background, your son's frame of mind, attitude of officials here, etc. When I got through that, I passed on what you'd told me. It seemed like the best place to start; the man I was talking to is a real insider.'

'CIA?' Keeper guessed.

Holman took a puff of his cigarette, let the question blow away with the smoke. 'He told me to bury it. He said he knew for a fact the woman was in Moscow. According to him, you must be a little overwrought.' Holman saw a pebble on the ground and gave it a resentful kick. 'I should've let it rest there, but I told you I'd check all the way through, so I did. We have a couple of troubleshooters at the Embassy; I phoned Moscow and put one of them on the job. Only the answer I got back didn't come from him. When I phoned again this evening I was put through to one of my superiors. He confirmed it – your way. Your wife is not anywhere in this country.'

'Where is she?'

Holman shook his head. 'We didn't get into that. Before I could ask any more questions I was told to forget about the whole thing, drop it cold or I'd be busted. On the subject of co-operating with Roy's chaperone, the orders were just as stiff: I do what he wants; when he whistles, I jump.' He looked sideways at Keeper. 'Now listen, I could've come back here and said everything was apple pie. In fact, those were my orders –'

'But you're doing me a special favour since we're such old chums. Come off it. Why the hell would you countermand orders for me?'

Holman raised his voice. 'Because they're the wrong damn orders. If the man who gave them ever meets you, he'll agree. You're a stubborn bastard, Keeper. If I don't level with you tonight, you'll be shooting your mouth off tomorrow when our correspondents come down to cover the trial, telling your story all over again. It's better this way.'

'Is it?' Keeper gave a mean growling laugh. 'You think I'll play dumb now, help you cover up her murder?'

'There's been no murder,' Holman snapped.

'Fit it together another way.'

Holman dragged deeply on the cigarette and flipped it into the sea. He watched the trail of sparks until it had died in the black water. 'I can't. But instead of information maybe you'll settle for advice: Let this scenario play out as it is. Your son's safety probably depends on it, and your wife's.'

'She isn't my wife any more,' Keeper said, thinking she wasn't alive any more either.

What were the lies protecting? From two sources now, Parritt and Holman, Keeper had gotten the feeling that not only the Russians were anxious for the exchange to go through.

Holman was looking sharply at Keeper. After a moment, he said quietly, 'I did find out a little more about Yolkin. Not very much, just what my friend in Moscow knew offhand. But it's enough to explain why the Russians won't be kind to Roy if this falls through. Although Yolkin is Russian, he was born in China and didn't come home until a couple of years before the Second World War. Since lately the Russians aren't getting along too well with the Chinese, they don't want to lose anyone with special insights into the oriental mind. There it is. I've run all your errands. Now I'm asking you a favour: Don't make trouble.'

Keeper glanced at Holman; with his crooked nose and worried eyes he looked like an honest conscionable boxer who had been told by his manager, only after the first bell, that the fix was in. Holman appeared to regret the machinations in which he was forced to participate, but clearly he believed there was no other way.

'I'm not asking for my own sake,' Holman added.

Keeper walked on silently for a minute, aware that Holman was watching constantly. At last, Keeper nodded.

Holman looked at his wristwatch. 'All right. Let's get back. We're being joined for dinner. Roy's bodyguard.' He shot an anxious glance at Keeper. 'It won't go down well if he learns I've talked to you this way.'

Keeper said nothing.

Holman shrugged. 'Let's take the dry way back.' He crossed over the promenade.

They walked past the café tables with their encampments of leathery-faced men. Most of them sat over drinks which they rarely touched, wistful eyes fixed on the night sea as if searching for a lantern on the horizon, the return of some lost love. Keeper and Holman were given momentary looks as they went by; then, catching sight of the man following alone at an un-varying twenty paces, the men at the tables turned away and took fast nervous sips from their glasses.

Would he keep his bargain with Holman, Keeper wondered. Could he justify co-operating solely on the basis of what he had learned about Yolkin? That explained why the Russians were pushing so hard and fast. But what was the reciprocal benefit? The book?

'What are we really getting out of this?' Keeper asked suddenly, studying Holman's reaction.

'Your son goes free.'

'That doesn't balance the equation, and you know it. Not on the scale of values you work by. There must be something else.'

Holman was silent.

'*The Mushroom Cave*, is that it?'

Holman walked on without answering. Finally, in a low voice, he said, 'I can't see how ... but it's the only thing I can figure. Somehow, even though he was caught, Roy connected. If we get him out, we'll have that book. And yet ... it doesn't seem possible. They must have gone over Roy. The Russians would never let that book just slip through ...'

'Maybe there's more to know about Yolkin,' Keeper said.

'If he was their top operator,' Holman argued, 'they still wouldn't trade for that book.'

125

'You really believe it's that valuable.'

'There are books that have changed the world,' Holman said. 'The Bible, *The Wealth of Nations*, *Uncle Tom's Cabin*, *Mein Kampf*, *Das Kapital*. It's a pretty short list, and the odds are that *The Mushroom Cave* wouldn't qualify. But the Kremlin can't afford to take the chance. The Russian people have always had a unique relationship with writers and the written word, a special respect. Name another country where poetry readings are held in stadiums before as many as seventy thousand people, or where there's a city like Gorki – a city of one million people named for a writer. Literature has helped to shape the history of this country, especially in the last hundred years. It was the great nineteenth-century writers – Gogol, Turgenyev, Tolstoy, Chekhov – whose agitation against the feudal system whipped up discontent in the masses until it exploded. Once the Commies were grateful to the intellectuals for helping them into power. Lenin thought Mayakovsky's revolutionary poems so effectively moved the people, he had them put up on a huge neon sign in Moscow, a different poem every month. But knowing about this influence, the system couldn't shake off a paranoid fear of the printed word. They've seen how it helped them, they know how much it could hurt. *The Mushroom Cave* would give its readers an inside view of the Soviet elite in its worst moments. Maybe that wouldn't change anything. But the leadership is scared as hell it would.'

'But how could it?' Keeper said. 'Here where it counts most it would have to be read in samizdat. It would take years to reach even a few thousand people. And they'd probably be spread all over the country. Even if *The Mushroom Cave* convinced them all that their government was bloody and corrupt, they couldn't simultaneously turn the last page and march on the Kremlin. By the time any concerted popular movement developed, the mob on top would have changed anyway; the guilty old men would be gone.'

'Logic's on your side,' Holman observed. 'But the Kremlin's fear isn't based on logic. They're scared of that book in a way that's almost ... superstitious.'

The word rang a bell. Culdiev had also mentioned the grip of superstition.

'There isn't much doubt, then,' Keeper said quietly, almost to himself. 'If the book exists, we'd stop at nothing to get it.'

They were crossing the plaza now, nearing the hotel. The man who was following took up his position again, leaning under the same palm tree as before.

'We'd do a hell of a lot,' Holman admitted. In front of the hotel entrance he stopped and faced Keeper. 'But I think we'd know where to draw the line.'

They went in. It was the first time Keeper had seen the lobby crowded. Clusters of men in dark suits stood in bored silence, their hands folded; a tour of undertakers waiting for their excursion bus to arrive.

Holman scanned apprehensively for the man they would be meeting. He snatched a look at his watch, his face relaxed.

'We're early,' he said. Subdued nods of recognition came at him from a couple of corners. He returned them.

'Who are they?' Keeper asked.

'Third Assistant Commissars for this and that, or so the introductions went. Press over there' – he faced towards a man with glasses and grey brilliantined hair – 'Transportation' – warts and black brilliantined hair – 'Culture' – bearish and jowly with a white crewcut.

'Come from the big town to see the show,' Keeper said acidly.

A racket of boot heels clacking militantly on the polished stone floor snapped Keeper's attention to the stairway. A Russian Army officer, old and square and arrogant enough to be of high rank, had just descended. He marched straight out through the lobby trailed by a couple of subordinates. The undertakers watched without a murmur; and suddenly Keeper realized that the lobby was pervaded not by the silence of boredom, but the repressed quiet of extreme tension. All eyes stayed on the Russian officer, who could be seen through the lobby door stepping into a khaki car with a large red star on the side.

'What gives?' Keeper said as the car pulled away.

Holman shook his head. He looked worried.

Voices floated down the stairwell, pulling glances away from the door. Two men appeared around the right-angle turn in the stairs and stopped on the landing, still in shadow from the knees up. Aware that they were being watched, the two men

127

dropped their voices and continued talking for another minute. Then they moved down into the light.

Even when the boyish features were clearly illuminated Keeper had to look twice. It was Parritt – talking with a blond, pipe-smoking man whose bushy eyebrows brimmed over gold-framed spectacles.

Parritt left his conversation and came over to them. Briskly, unceremoniously, he said, 'Hello, Keeper,' and then switched his attention to Holman. 'You're taking over here. Get Keeper his tickets out, etcetera. You'll get full co-operation from the other side with anything you need. I think the AP and UPI boys have already arrived; they're booked into another hotel nearer the port, The Georgian. Get over there now and tell them the trial's off. It wouldn't hurt if you got them on the first train or plane out of here, but don't push it. Just tell them they're missing the hot end of the story, in Moscow.'

Before either Holman or Keeper could react, Parritt was walking away. There were no good-byes. Holman showed a mask of utter confusion to Keeper, then turned to watch Parritt rejoin the pipe-smoking man as they left the hotel and clambered into a black car. It shot away, tyres squealing. Within seconds the close purr of a siren had faded to a distant bawl.

Holman left Keeper and went over to one of his Russian acquaintances. He returned after a brief, intense exchange. 'It comes out the same in Russian. No trial. They took Roy from prison an hour ago and put him on a plane for Moscow. The deal had to go through faster, I guess. The world will have to judge Roy on a signed confession.'

'Your contribution,' Keeper said tightly.

'Yeah,' Holman said, his voice hardly more than a whisper. 'Well, you heard the man; I've got work. I'll see you later. Meanwhile, you can grab dinner; there's a place across the square.' He left abruptly, and Keeper found himself swapping stares with the undertakers.

After a moment, he went up to his room. Though he hadn't eaten all day, he had lost his appetite.

Going Home

He had been wrong to pull at the loose threads in the curtain that separated him from the truth. Foolishly, he had expected the threads to be short extraneous ends, to come away leaving the fabric whole and neat. Instead, they didn't end, became more unsightly as they were pulled out, the fabric unravelled. And now Keeper felt he wasn't prepared to see what stood behind the curtain. He had been told outright that his interference could do nothing but harm. Perhaps he had seen the proof that his movements affected some tender balance. The acceleration in the exchange schedule might be connected with his visit to Culdiev. If the Russians knew about it, could guess what Keeper had been told, they might have feared the exchange would be exposed as a setup, aborted before the transaction was completed.

Or had they eavesdropped on Holman's phone calls to Moscow? Was it the chance that Susan's presence there would be challenged that had frightened them, threatened their scenario? But why? They weren't the authors of that deception.

He had to stop. Stop asking questions, pushing for explanations. For the moment it might have worked to Roy's advantage. But if he went on he might touch the wrong nerve, touch off a deadly reflex. Keeper regretted having let Holman go without first clarifying arrangements to get himself out of the country.

He pulled a chair onto the terrace, into the sultry air. A murmur of voices rose from below as the men in dark suits trickled out of the hotel and were driven away in black sedans. Keeper tried to keep his mind a blank, watching the pinpricks of light that glided across the black screen, ships far out on the sea. But images rose into his thoughts, unbidden from opaque depths like bubbles of marsh gas:

Parritt in the lobby, his face marked by worry, mouth tight, eyes almost twitching.

Parritt getting into the car with the other man, the car racing away, tyres in a squealing spin, siren screaming. Notes of emergency.

It didn't add up. Parritt had been sent to escort Roy – a priority assignment, to judge from Holman's deference. But Roy had been released from prison and put on a plane out of Batumi an hour before Parritt left the hotel. Surely the Russians hadn't deliberately thwarted Parritt in the performance of his duty. The reciprocal use of bodyguards was part of the deal; departing from the agreement might void the exchange. There were other indications that the Russians had been caught off balance: the anxiety Keeper had seen in the faces of the bureaucrats and military men.

He began to feel something like seasickness, as if his bodily equilibrium could be upset by the attempt to balance facts for which there was no centre, no logic. Perhaps it was only the need for food. He went to the phone and, using the phrase book Holman had supplied, requested something to eat, anything.

Half an hour later a stooped old man arrived carrying a tray with a bowl of viscous white soup and a plate on which were three slices of coarse bread. As Keeper took the tray and made a reflex move to find a tip, he recalled the young bell-boy. Was the old man also linked to Culdiev's group? Keeper could send a message that the trial had been cancelled. It was a short-lived impulse to stay in the game. Let Culdiev find for himself.

The old man smiled greedily as he watched Keeper's hand come out of his pocket. Keeper chuckled too, as he selected two quarters from the handful of American coins. He would be leaving Russia without ever having seen or touched its money, without having done so much as unpack his bag.

This time the tip was accepted, the old porter's gratitude approaching awe. He stood for a minute peering into his palm, then held one quarter up in each of his knobby hands and turned them around slowly in the light. His eyes travelled from the small silver moons down to Keeper.

'Vash. Eentun,' he said.

Keeper nodded automatically, unwilling to frisk his phrase book for the appropriate response.

'*Vasheen. Tun.*' The old man pointed to the portrait on one of the coins as he backed towards the open door. At the threshold he swiped one hand furiously through the air with a chopping motion. '*Vishnyak!*' he added, breaking into a phlegmy laugh as he pulled the door shut.

Cherry tree, Keeper supposed.

When he finished eating, he kept another hour's vigil for Holman, then got into bed. Holding his eyes closed, he told himself sleep was near. But he was a long time backing down the tunnel, reading a graffiti of names, the words of Susan's letter, the title of an unpublished book by a dead man.

During the night he woke, a strange total waking. His eyes were already on the door when they opened, his ears tuned acutely to the sound of footsteps retreating in the outside corridor. Ghosts of sounds made while he slept lingered in the corners of the room. A knock on the door, a few words called out, part of a conversation overheard. He considered running after the footsteps, but they were gone before he decided that he didn't want to know what they had come to tell him. Keeper closed his eyes and was immediately asleep again.

The next knock came early. A fingernail of sun was clawing the ridges of the Caucasian peaks; the sea mirrored a sky of baby-blanket pink.

Holman didn't move through the door. 'You're up. Good. Packed?'

'I never unpacked.'

'Let's go.'

Keeper guessed Holman had not been to sleep. His eyes were red, his complexion bloodless.

'Slow down, Holman, I'm not baggage. I won't be bundled out on any ticket you hand me.'

'Shut up.' Holman's tone was incongruously gentle. He sighed and came into the room reluctantly. He had wanted to wait at least until they were on their way.

He stood with his head down, back to Keeper. 'Your son's dead.'

131

Keeper stared. 'What?'

'He did it himself. Cut his throat with a razor. Last night on the –'

With two quick steps Keeper had reached Holman. Savagely gripping his shoulder he spun him around. 'What kind of shit are you all handing out? Tell me now. Tell me or so help me God, I'll –'

'I'm telling you what I know, Keeper!'

'Bastards. What do you take me for? He was getting out. Why would he kill himself?' Keeper shivered with rage, a rage without grief that kept his heart cold even as the blood rammed through it. 'They found the book, didn't they?'

Holman shook his head. 'No, that wouldn't cover it. Even if they had, they'd want Roy alive. More than ever. He'd have information, about his contacts, the channels. And after they got it out of him, he might still be good for a deal on Yolkin. The Russians are the losers because of this; the ones I've dealt with are as shocked as we are.' Holman gripped Keeper's hand and dragged it down from his shoulder. 'Maybe he was thrown by those few days in gaol,' he went on quietly. 'That particular place would depress anyone, the strongest ... and, well, he'd used LSD, hadn't he? Nobody knows the latent effects of that stuff.'

Keeper turned away. 'Parritt knew this last night. This is why the trial was called off.'

'No. They didn't tell us until three o'clock this morning. I came and knocked at your door. You slept through it.'

'That story about Roy flying out – why did they stall?'

'They didn't. The story was true – he was going home. That's the craziest part. He was already on his way, the plane was in the air when he did it, halfway to Moscow.'

'You said it was the prison –'

'I said it might have started a depression he couldn't shake.'

'Crap.'

Holman sank onto the room's plain chair and lit a cigarette. For a minute they didn't speak.

'Where's Parritt?' Keeper said at last.

'I haven't seen him since he left here last night,' Holman replied wearily. 'But look, Keeper, he wouldn't know any more.

This was a suicide. We know for certain the Russians had put Roy on the plane; our two news-service correspondents saw him go. When I connected with them last night they were just coming back from a junket to a military airfield near here; they'd been allowed to cover Roy's take-off, even talked to him before he boarded the plane.' Holman reached into his jacket and brought out several folded sheets of yellow paper. 'It's all there,' he said, handing them to Keeper.

The story was written in pencil. The sheets of paper, lined, with Russian printing on top, looked like telegraph submission forms. It was the happy ending to Roy's stay in Batumi, the story that would never be printed:

BATUMI, Oct. 24 –

Roy Keeper, the 22-year-old American accused of spying and anti-Soviet propaganda activities, was released tonight from the Russian prison where he had been confined for one week. The charges against Keeper arose from an alleged attempt to receive an unpublished manuscript by Semyon Lyndushkin, the Russian writer who died last year in a Soviet prison camp.

Keeper was taken under heavy guard to a military airfield where he boarded a flight for Moscow. Looking strained and nervous from his ordeal, Keeper nevertheless smiled when asked how he felt to be going home, and said: 'Are you kidding, man? It's like Christmas.'

To secure Keeper's release, the United States had agreed to return Pavel Yolkin, the Russian trade official arrested last 29 June by the FBI. Yolkin has since been awaiting trial on spy charges.

An official spokesman at the U.S. Embassy in Moscow said Yolkin would arrive there tomorrow evening, after which Keeper would be free to leave. He was expected to fly to Paris where he has been living. The Embassy spokesman admitted that Keeper's release prior to trial had come as a surprise. A conviction against Keeper would have given Russian authorities a valuable weapon in their battle with dissident intellectual activity. By establishing the precedent that foreign nationals who handle banned literary material are liable to charges of espionage, Russian citizens responsible for the creation and distribution of such material would, by implication, be subject to charges of treason. Cancellation of the trial suggests, however, that the Government is at present reluctant to put this strategy to a test.

Some Kremlinologists have suggested that Keeper's prompt

release is a conciliating move to further passage of the East-West trade bill scheduled to come before Congress within the next two weeks.

Keeper refolded the several sheets of paper and dropped them on Holman's lap. Then he went out to the terrace and, facing the sea, sucked in the breeze as though it were a tranquillizing medicine. There was so much that stank; he could never accept that Roy's death had been suicide.

But why should Roy be killed? If *The Mushroom Cave* was merely legend, then an opportunity had been destroyed that the Russians had worked months to create. If the book really did exist, if Roy had managed to conceal it for a while – on microfilm, perhaps, as a microdot – Holman was right that Roy would be even more valuable after the book was discovered.

Unless it hadn't actually been found! Keeper thought through the story of Folscha's approach, the conditions that had been laid down. If Folscha was genuine, then the student arrested at the Botanical Gardens had known the book's true hiding place. The student might have been put in the same prison as Roy; personally, or feeding it through the grapevine, he might have told Roy the hiding place. And the Russians, fearing that Roy would pass the secret back along the samizdat network after his release, had decided that keeping the book hidden was more important to the survival of the regime than one run-of-the-mill spy.

It was at least a more likely account of Roy's death than suicide.

Keeper went back into the room. 'It's murder,' he said. 'They murdered him.'

His definitive tone drew a penetrating glare from Holman. But Keeper didn't amplify the statement. This wasn't the time or place to confide what he knew about Folscha and Culdiev. For that matter, was Holman someone he could safely talk to? He had thought so. But Holman was too ready to hush things up, play ball with the boys in the head office.

Holman's glare cooled. He stood. 'The body was flown back as far as Tiflis. They want you there to make an identification.' After a moment, he picked up Keeper's suitcase and waited by the door for Keeper to precede him out.

There was a car in front of the hotel, again with a Red Army driver. Another was parked behind it. No helicopter this time; no photographer to record Keeper's departure. They were as anxious to sneak him away as they had been to fanfare his arrival.

The car headed inland, driving up sharply graded streets of old wooden houses that reminded Keeper of San Francisco.

Twenty minutes' driving brought them to a military airfield on the outskirts of the city. The same, Keeper imagined, from which Roy had left. The car turned through sentried gates and went down a mile of runway to where a two-engine propeller plane was revving up.

There was a short ramp ascending to the plane door. At the bottom, Holman grabbed Keeper by the sleeve. 'Keeper, I want a word with you.' He strained to control his voice, trying to be heard over the airplane motors without shouting too loud.

Over Holman's shoulder Keeper watched a man get out of the second car and walk towards them. Stringbean. He came up to Holman and said something in polite Russian. Holman answered politely. Then Stringbean touched Holman's elbow and tried to steer him up the ramp. Frisking loose, Holman shouted angrily at Stringbean, who looked back in mute astonishment; then, with a philosophic dip of his head, the Russian walked away. Holman waited until he saw Stringbean engaged in conversation with the driver of his car, then turned to Keeper.

'I want to make sure you know this: There's one hell of a responsibility riding on you. Start throwing wild accusations in the wrong places and the damage you do could be fantastic.'

'We're on the way to the morgue,' Keeper said snidely, 'and you're still worried about being the good little diplomat.'

'That's how it is,' Holman replied evenly. 'If you call this murder – to their faces, or anytime after you leave here – it can't do anything but harm. So get that idea out of your head, or keep it to yourself.'

'I don't know. Would Parritt give me the same advice? A couple of days ago he was telling me about the value of propaganda. Wouldn't this be a gold mine?'

Holman frowned. 'Parritt comes out of a different shop. They've got their job to do and their way of doing it. But it's only one way. We're trying to build bridges – that's where the hope is.'

'Really noble. But there's a body or two lying in the middle of this bridge. What about that? What if it was murder?'

'Keeper, there isn't a reason –'

'The book,' Keeper said quickly. 'Isn't that reason enough?'

'It would be,' Holman replied, 'only if Roy had every word memorized. If by killing him they erased the words. That's not possible.'

'No. But it's something like that,' Keeper said emphatically.

Holman studied Keeper. 'What do you know . . .?'

Keeper hesitated. 'It's a feeling, that's all.'

'Not good enough.'

'Not for you.' Keeper moved towards the ramp.

Holman blocked his way. 'Goddamn you, Keeper, there's more than your precious feelings at stake, You've got to cool it.'

'Cool it. Sit tight. Lie down. Play dead!' Keeper's voice jumped volume with each phrase. 'That's all I've heard. And there's always a good reason. National interest. International brotherhood. But what about justice, straight old-fashioned justice? Isn't anyone trying to protect that?'

Holman stayed calm. 'There's only one kind of justice possible at this level. We'll outlast them – that'll be justice.'

'I can't wait that long.'

Keeper shoved Holman aside and climbed the first two steps of the ramp. Then Holman caught him, pushed him brutally against the metal protecting rail. The top of it slammed into Keeper's kidneys. Pain sliced him in half.

Holman held Keeper against the rail. 'You can't wait, can you? Can't wait to unload the guilt. I'll tell you why you can't believe it was suicide. Because then you helped to kill him. Who knows? A word from you, some kind of encouragement, and –'

'They wouldn't let me see him. You told me –'

'And Jack Keeper does what he's told,' Holman scoffed. 'Why didn't you throw your weight around? Even the Russians are impressed with millionaires. You might have gotten in. Anyway, you could have sent him a note. Even trying to get through would have meant something.'

'Easy to say now what I should have done. But I didn't know when I came that he had only one more day to live.' Keeper struggled to free himself, but Holman wouldn't yield. Then Keeper rammed his forearm hard up under Holman's chin, pressed against the throat. Choking, Holman gave way, took a gulp of air, then lunged forward . . .

But Stringbean had run between them. With all the strength of his thin arms he levered the two Americans apart. He stood between them, panting, as they glared at each other.

'Saved by the K G B,' Keeper said finally .

Holman laughed. Then Keeper joined in, and they laughed together, short crackling laughs that ended before they reached the top of the ramp.

Symptom

Keeper came down the ramp first, several steps ahead of Holman. During the short flight they had sat in separate rows, not speaking, moodily sipping the gritty coffee Stringbean served from a thermos.

He recognized the man waiting at the bottom of the ramp. The pipe-smoking academic type who had left the hotel with Parritt last night. Like Holman, the man seemed to have spent a sleepless night. His shoulders sloped defeatedly, a shadow of stubble lined his chin.

The greeting was solemn. 'Mr Keeper, I am Gavril Schub. My government authorizes me to extend on its behalf the deepest condolences for this tragedy. It is sincerely hoped that you will not confuse events of last night with measures previously taken by the Soviet Union to enforce its national policies. Your son's suicide is regrettable for all concerned.'

Keeper did not accept the ceremonially proffered handshake. 'Show me the body,' he said wearily.

Schub shifted his eyes past Keeper. 'You are Mr Holman?'

Holman nodded and came down beside Keeper.

'I have instructions,' said Schub, 'to co-operate with you in expediting transport and other matters pertaining to a proper and respectful dispensation of the remains. We will defer to Mr Keeper's wishes in the highest degree possible. Convey them to me without hesitation.' He turned back to Keeper. 'You may, of course, go at once to make identification. But ... have you had breakfast? Something would be advisable ...'

'I've met you on an empty stomach,' Keeper muttered. 'I should be able to manage the rest.'

Holman reddened. But Schub gave a wry dispassionate shrug and led the way to the first of two black cars, the standard cortege. He stood by as Keeper and Holman got into the back seat, then seated himself in front and nodded to the driver.

It was the same straight highway that Keeper had ridden his first night in Russia. By day the high mountains hemming it in provided spectacular scenery. He pretended to be absorbed in it.

Holman, wanting to give some sign of support, launched the inquiry:

'I haven't been able to tell Mr Keeper very much about the circumstances of his son's death. Exactly what happened?'

Schub was lighting his pipe. He sucked at the flame until it had gone deep into the tobacco. Then from a briefcase he extracted a thin dossier. Opening it, he referred to the top page, then recited: 'At a few minutes before eight o'clock yesterday evening the prisoner was released from detention and taken under guard to the airport. In consideration of your government's prompt acceptance of conditions for his release, it was decided not to unnecessarily stigmatize the boy by a trial. A further point in his favour was the confession.' He glanced again at the report. 'The boy arrived at the airport at eight-seventeen. Before entering the aircraft, he paused to talk with your newsmen.'

Keeper smiled sourly at the delicate refinements in Schub's narrative. Roy had been 'the prisoner' first, then 'the boy'; an intimation that his freedom had been restored before he died, that if he was still under guard it was a protective courtesy he had snubbed by killing himself.

Schub took a piece of lined yellow paper from the dossier and passed it to Holman. 'A copy of the news transmission filed before the tragedy.'

The tragedy. Another neat fillip of heartfelt sympathy, Keeper mused.

Holman finished reading and handed Keeper the paper. The story had undergone a few changes.

BATUM. Oct. 24

Roy Keeper, the 22-year-old American accused of spying and anti-Soviet activities, was released tonight and taken to an airfield where he boarded a flight to Moscow. He will be exchanged for Pavel Yolkin, the Russian trade official the United States has held in custody for four months. Keeper's release prior to trial is seen as a conciliating move towards easing East-West relations.

'You may keep it,' Schub said when Keeper held out the sheet of paper.

'For my scrapbook.' Keeper balled the paper in his fist and dropped it on the floor.

'Go on,' Holman said quickly. 'What time did the plane take off?'

Schub looked at the report. 'Eight twenty-nine.'

'Who was on board?'

'The boy, a crew of two, and a guard contingent of twelve.'

'Twelve men to guard one?'

Schub nodded, but offered no explanation.

Keeper remained silent, waiting to see how hard Holman would push.

'That's a very heavy guard,' Holman said.

'Heavy?' Schub smiled. 'What protection is too much in these days of hijacking? We had given our word to deliver the boy. We were doing our best to keep that promise.'

'Not quite,' Holman said. 'One of our men was supposed to be on that flight. But he was at the hotel with you a half hour after the plane took off.'

Schub puffed on his pipe. His next words were a long time in coming, perhaps because they contravened the doctrine of Communist infallibility. 'The plane's embarkation without Mr Parritt was a mistake. It arose from good intentions, our haste to conclude the exchange so the boy could return home. All the same, it was an error, a simple oversight in briefing the pilot. We made every effort to correct it.'

'How?' Holman asked.

'The pilot was instructed by radio to land at the airport to which he was then nearest. A second plane dispatched Mr Parritt to make the connection. When you saw us last night I was taking him to board this plane.'

That reinforced what Keeper had sensed: that the Russians had been co-operating with Parritt to get him somewhere fast. But the tension in the hotel lobby; the look on the Commissar's faces, had been generated by something more than a 'simple oversight'. It had been the electric gloom of power brokers awaiting the latest bulletins about a palace coup.

'As instructed,' Schub continued, 'the first plane flew on to the nearest safe landing site. This was the civil airport at Kharkov, another half hour away. During this time the boy asked permission to use the lavatory. There was no objection. As the landing at Kharkov grew imminent and the boy had not returned, one of the guards went to get him. The tragedy was then discovered.'

'Time?'

'Twenty minutes after nine.'

'And he was already dead?'

'We believe so.'

'You aren't sure?' Holman asked quickly.

'As you know,' Schub replied evenly, 'lavatory compartments on aircraft are quite small. In falling, the body had wedged against the door; it could be opened only a crack, not enough to see exactly what had occurred. The guards thought that the boy had fainted, and did not force the door as this might have done injury. Unfortunately, a few moments were wasted. However, when some blood flowed under the door into view, it was immediately broken down.' Schub shuffled through the dossier to one of the bottom papers. 'The medical report states unequivocally that, in any case, the boy could not have survived more than a minute or two after inflicting the wound.' He glanced piercingly at Keeper, a dare to join the interrogation.

Holman also surrendered the lead. 'I can't think of anything else.'

Finally Keeper said, 'It sounds like Roy was treated very decently. I mean, not every prisoner' – he pointedly restored the term – 'would be allowed to have a sharp instrument like a razor in his possession.'

'That's right.' Holman sat forward. 'He told me it wasn't allowed.'

'Of course,' Keeper went on, 'aboard the plane there was a more relaxed atmosphere. So relaxed there were twelve men to watch Roy's every move.'

'I think,' said Schub patiently, 'you have misunderstood the duties of our guards. Remember, please, that your son was allied to certain ... misguided elements in this country: a small group, but energetic. They might have used the boy's arrival in Moscow as the occasion for a demonstration, an attempt to attract widespread attention to their opinions. Our twelve men were a precaution – the insulation, shall we say, to separate the spark from the explosive.' He glanced mischievously at Holman. 'Surely you understand? Do you not, once in a great while, have demonstrations in your own country?'

Holman ignored the sarcasm. 'You've answered half the question. What about the razor?'

'Indeed. I was coming to that.' Schub responded eagerly, like a student who had prepared well for an examination. 'Let us be clear he had not, in fact, a razor; merely a blade. This was concealed from us. Though even if we had provided him a razor on the plane, we should accept no guilt. The boy was on his way to a happy resolution. Why should we suspect he would turn on himself? In the prison, yes, we guard against these things. But under the circumstances, the boy's concealment of the blade was itself a ... symptom ...'

Symptom of what? Schub's inferences were plain. Instability. Psychotic behaviour. Death wish. But was it Roy's mania, Keeper wondered, that had made him cling to some sort of weapon? Or had he needed protection against the obsession of other men to bury a secret?

Keeper said no more, just traded cold stares with Schub. And he felt a stupid juvenile thrill when Schub turned away first, pretended annoyance with his pipe and busied himself repacking it.

The ride ended in front of a low monolithic building, the last on a street that ran straight from the city's central river to the base of a high mountain. Running up the mountainside was a funicular railway. As Keeper got out of the car, Schub pointed with his pipestem to the summit of the mountain. 'There is wonderful view from the top,' said Schub. More of the Chamber of Commerce patter he had begun as they drove into the city, naming various places along their route, reeling off dull statistics: 'That is the Academy of Agricultural Sciences. The city boasts two hundred research institutions ...' The gloss of geniality vanished abruptly, however, as they passed into the building. Schub stopped at a booth and presented his credentials to a pair of armed guards. The other Russians in the escort also identified themselves; then all but Stringbean disappeared into corridors and elevators running from the cavernous main entrance hall.

Schub, Stringbean, Holman and Keeper got into an elevator together. Stringbean pressed a button. The illuminated control panel showed them descending to five levels below the surface. They emerged into a long narrow corridor with rough walls of unfinished concrete. The air was heavy with moisture. In the dim light of widely spaced bulbs there was an illusion of being outside in a desolate street on a rainy night. Halos encircled the naked bulbs. Beads of water gathered on the stone walls and dripped onto the floor.

The corridor ended at a metal double door. Schub paused. 'Perhaps, Mr Keeper, you would like first a few minutes alone?'

Keeper shook his head.

The morgue was approximately a hundred feet long and half as wide, with ice-white tiled walls soaring thirty or forty feet to a ceiling painted grey. Keeper had the feeling he had stepped into a glacial Siberian ravine. Perhaps the suggestion had been engineered into the morgue's design; death, it said, was just one more province on the far fringe of Siberia, not another world beyond the State's jurisdiction. The capacity for bodies was enormous. Tiers of body lockers were built into the walls. In each of the four corners were ladders giving access to catwalks for attending to the upper tiers.

On the highest catwalk a man stepped forward and leaned over the rail like a bored sailor staring into the ocean from the deck of a moving ship. He had exchanged so many looks with the dead he seemed to have lost the knack of looking at the living.

A few minutes alone, Schub had offered. But the watching man came as no surprise to Keeper. They never left you completely alone – he knew that now.

Behind the man on the catwalk one of the lockers was pulled out from the wall. And tied to the rail where the man stood was a rope-and-pulley system; it hung down to the floor and connected to a wooden platform. The crude rig, which could be shuttled around the rail, evidently served to raise and lower bodies. Keeper savoured the irony: the huge morgue, testament to the treacheries of modern power, served at its heart by a peasant device.

A slight rustle of fabric whispered across the room. Schub had moved to the far corner, was standing there by a table, one hand raised with peculiar grace holding the corner of a sheet. He stood motionless as Keeper approached.

The crescent slash under the jaw was the first thing Keeper noticed. No pains had been taken to cosmetically camouflage the wound, mute the grisly effect. It had been laced shut in blatant crisscross stitches with coarse black thread. Keeper stared at the lurid lacing.

'Who did that?'

'I don't know.' Schub appeared puzzled that this should be a matter of concern. 'This is your son, Mr Keeper?'

How much like the newspaper pictures he looked, Keeper thought. Then, like a scene glimpsed through the window of a speeding train, he saw a riverbank in the sun; Roy, fourteen, winding in a fish. Keeper felt a timid sadness, not grief but nostalgia. It passed and he felt absurd: to be caring now, so long after the death of possibilities. He didn't belong here making this identification, mourning. Where was she?

'Well, sir, you will verify this is your son?' Schub's hand was still poised daintily in midair, pressuring for a reply.

Keeper whisked the sheet from Schub's grasp, exposing the upper part of the torso. It had been only rebellion against Schub's impatience, not investigation. But when the arms and chest were bared, Keeper saw the bruises.

'Look at this,' Keeper said quickly to Holman, who had been standing back a few feet.

There was one on the chest, near the armpit. Not the roundish blotch that would have come from a bump, a blow, but a line about three inches long and a quarter inch wide, running laterally towards the nipple. Keeper could think of a couple of possible causes: the blade of a knife pressed with great force through a layer of clothing, or a strand of rope tied very tightly. There were also three smaller bruises along the left arm nearest to Keeper.

'Well?' Holman said gravely to Schub.

The Russian had his reports out again. He read to himself for a moment. 'Yes, I see,' he mumbled and lowered the paper. 'I have told you force was required to enter the lavatory. The line on the chest is where the edge of the door struck the body at that time. The bruises on the arm may have been caused in the same way, or when the boy fell.'

Keeper hesitated, then flung the sheet fully away from the table. As it billowed up and sailed onto the floor the sickly sweet smell of formaldehyde filled the air. Slowly Keeper began circling the table, looking for other bruises around the ankles, the ribs, the other arm. Schub watched impassively. Stringbean lounged by the door, whistling softly; the sound carried across the vast echoing morgue. Keeper saw no other marks until he came around to the other side of Roy's face. There, just over the cheekbone under the eye, was a small raw crater in the flesh ringed by a blue ridge. The skin had been gouged somehow, not punctured.

Schub was already consulting his papers. '. . . also when he fell . . . a small valve screw at the floor of the compartment . . .'

Keeper thought of the plane in which he had flown from Istanbul. The interior had not been as sleek as an American jet's. Even so, he doubted any of a plane's systems were left exposed in lavatory corners.

Schub droned on. '. . . thus striking into the skin . . .'

'You've got answers for everything,' Keeper muttered.

'Is that a criticism, Mr Keeper? I do, after all, owe you an explanation.'

There was a silence.

A pinpoint of white dropped from high above, made a sound as it hit the floor. Keeper looked at it, a cigarette stub thrown down by the man on the catwalk. He glanced to Holman.

'You believe it?'

Holman shrugged awkwardly. 'It's possible.'

'Shit,' Keeper hissed. Moving past Holman to plant himself in front of Schub, he said, 'I think it's a cigarette burn; I think Roy was tortured.'

'Jesus,' Holman murmured. He turned to Schub with a wordless gesture of apology.

Schub's eyes blazed, his voice quavered with anger. 'I shall give you the benefit of the doubt, Mr Keeper, and presume your judgement is clouded by emotion.'

'The benefit of the doubt – you'll give me . . . ?'

'Keeper!' Holman leapt forward, but to late to intervene.

Keeper felt the scrape of teeth on his knuckles as his fist jarred Schub's mouth open. Then Stringbean was beside him, breathing hard, the cold metal of his gun barrel pressing into Keeper's temple.

'Go ahead, tell him to shoot,' Keeper goaded Schub, who sat on the floor, dazed, rubbing his jaw. 'Holman here will swear it was suicide.'

'I just might, Keeper. You make it damn hard to be on the same side.'

Schub struggled to his feet looking mystified but unrevengeful, like a child fallen from a seesaw. Holman lent him support and said, 'I'm sorry about this.'

'Now get out your whisk broom and dust him off,' Keeper said caustically.

Holman ignored it. 'I think we can resolve this reasonably,' he said to Schub. 'Tell your man to put away his gun.'

'No,' Schub said. 'We will leave things as they are while I try to make sense with this madman.' He came up to Keeper. 'Your son –' He stopped and looked at the body, still lying naked. Picking up the sheet from the floor, Schub arranged it neatly over the corpse, then resumed. 'Your son committed suicide. Witnesses and the findings of examination by doctors attest to the fact. But you have a different opinion. Very well, Mr Keeper. Perhaps you would like another examination to be made, a complete autopsy for evidence of internal injuries, traces of poison. We have no objection.'

'Why should you? Would any of your examiners change his mind?'

'I have already said we will co-operate to transport the body wherever you wish. There you can make your own arrangements.'

'That's fair enough,' Holman put in.

Keeper was silent. There was a hitch, he was sure.

Schub gestured Stringbean to put away his gun. 'Then we are through here ... ?'

Keeper scanned the contours of the shrouded body and turned away.

'Good,' said Schub. 'We will go upstairs. I have some effects of the boy for you, Mr Keeper. And there are papers to sign.'

That was it. Papers. The body would not be released until he had signed forms, in effect endorsing the Russian medical report. Whatever any future autopsy determined, the issue would always be fudged by producing this corroboration. And if he refused to sign the papers, they would gladly agree to another examination on their own territory, another and another, always with the same results.

As they walked to the door, the man from the catwalk shinnied down one of the corner ladders. It was his soft whistling, not Stringbean's, that Keeper had heard. The man went on whistling the same tune as he set about transferring the body to the wooden platform.

A noise like the shrill chirping of terrified birds haunted the dank corridor outside the morgue – the straining squeak of the pulleys raising Roy back to the unfelt preserving chill.

Siamese Twins

Schub had not lied. There was a good view.

The mountaintop restaurant was a round glassed-in aerie where luxury and seediness managed to coexist. The plates and glassware all bore the name of the restaurant in gilt (Holman translated it as 'The Eagle's Nest'). And there were scrupulously clean damask napkins. But the tablecloths bore greasy stains as did the lapels of the waiters' white coats; and the food was poor: grilled slabs of lamb with a rough sour red wine.

It was obviously one of the better places. The parties of men eating and talking with gusto looked like the upper echelon of local bureaucrats and business commissars.

Keeper dawdled over his meal and gazed apathetically at the inescapable view. He had submitted without enthusiasm to Holman's suggestion to have lunch here. Still, he recognized the virtue of Holman's reasoning; this touch of a normal world, a normal day, might restore perspective. He had signed the papers to release the body, but there remained other blanks to be filled in, shipping orders for the coffin. And choosing the final destination had stymied him. The choice of a burial ground was supposed to be guided by sentiment, some sense of the fitness of place. But should Roy go into the earth of America after refusing to fight its wars? Lie where nobody would mourn him? Or in Paris? He had been living there. Perhaps there was someone who would lay fresh flowers on the grave, for a few weeks anyway. Certainly Roy had met someone in the city whom he trusted, someone who had earned the confidence essential to enlist him for the mission. But that someone might be the K G B plant who had delivered Roy for sacrifice.

Except to request salt or butter, Keeper and Holman did not speak until they were halfway through coffee.

Then Holman said, 'Those bruises, the small hole in his cheek

'... they could have happened the way we were told. But they ought to be looked at again.' Keeper turned from the cottony blue horizon of mountains and looked guardedly at Holman, who took a sip of his coffee and continued. 'I thought so as soon as I saw the body. But what if I had joined in the shouting, or started throwing punches?' He nodded at the nearby table where Stringbean sat with his fat companion. 'His gun might have gone off. And there's enough strain over what's already happened.'

'Still worrying about cosy relations with the Russians,' Keeper said tightly.

Holman put a spoon in his half-empty coffee cup and stirred, pointlessly; he had not added cream or sugar. 'I want to help you. I haven't felt right about what we're doing in this since you told me about the boy's mother. Last night after I heard she wasn't really in Moscow, it preyed on me. On top of that, what's happened to Roy . . .' His voice faded, he shook his head. 'But it dies hard – believing that we can talk to them, that there are ways to avoid the killing. This kind of thing makes it all seem so hopeless.'

'You talk as if they broke a promise,' Keeper said, 'as if they were always good before. Don't forget what *The Mushroom Cave* is supposedly about, the wholesale bloodletting, murderers right at the top. You can't expect any better from them now.'

Holman stared bleakly at Keeper. His lips trembled like an old man's, as though forming the words took an accumulation of will, a piling up of synapses. 'From us, Keeper, I expect better from us. That's why I'll help.'

Keeper reacted slowly. 'What are you saying? Who do you think killed Roy?'

'I don't know.' A note of agony came through Holman's whisper. 'Anything is possible.'

'But we agreed to the exchange.'

'We.' Holman lingered over the word. 'It sounds so neat when you say it, so solid. But "we" is an animal with many heads; they don't all think alike.'

A phrase slipped out of Keeper's memory. 'Their job to do ... their way of doing it.' Holman had been speaking of Parritt: Parritt who had disappeared, Parritt whose movements

Holman had tried to pin down when questioning Schub, Parritt who had proclaimed the almighty value of propaganda. As Keeper had realized earlier, any suspicion that the Russians had murdered Roy (and it would creep inevitably into Western news coverage) could be a propaganda gold mine. Opened with the same stroke that deprived the Russians of their purchased spy. If the book didn't exist, then this was the answer. Look at the balance sheet: Who had gained most by Roy's death? And who had lost?

'Parritt,' Keeper said, 'he did it, didn't he?'

Holman gulped the last of his cold coffee. 'Wild guesses won't do any good. I can't say any more without something tangible to go on.'

'Can you get it?'

'I'm going to try. There might be a clue somewhere in our files.' Holman studied a grease spot on the tablecloth like a fortune teller reading signs of the future. 'Spying, Keeper. That's what it comes down to. To find out anything I'll have to dig into stuff that's marked "secret". I'm ready. If we've come to this it has to be stopped. But you'll have to do your part.'

'Which is?'

'You're the outlet. If I come up with anything significant I'll funnel it to you.'

'I don't care about making headlines. If you get the evidence, blow the whistle yourself. I'll be satisfied.'

'You don't understand,' Holman said. 'If there's a story to tell it can never come from the inside. The damage couldn't be localized. That's why even the most decent insiders, if any of them know, will sit on it forever.'

'Then what does that make you?'

'The front-line man, the man who met your son, who saw him alive and then dead and can't just write him off as a necessary casualty; who thinks that, maybe, for the sake of some principle we've started selling our souls. Of course I could be wrong. Maybe the casualty was necessary. But how would I know? I'm a diplomat, a servant of compromise. The facts have to be seen by someone still capable of judging them, someone outside, impartial –'

'That lets me out,' Keeper said flatly.

'If I come up with something,' Holman persisted, 'I think you're as good as anybody to decide whether to use it.'

'I'm not impartial,' Keeper stressed. 'Give me proof that Roy was killed by our own people so we could pick up a few points in some ideological popularity poll, and I'll use it. And how I'll use it!'

Holman hesitated, then pushed the salt and pepper shakers, two glass vials with metal tops, to the centre of the table. He arranged the vials tightly together. 'Siamese twins. What do you do with them? They live off one heart, a shared system of organs. But their personalities are different. One is reasonable, slow-moving, pretty honest, a little flabby. The other is rash, secretive, belligerent, and well-muscled. The twins make our policies, Keeper. It may seem like a good idea to separate them, until you've got the knife in your hand. Because there's always a chance with Siamese twins that if you cut, they'll both die.' Holman slid the handle of a spoon between the vials and gave it a sharp twist; both shakers toppled over. 'There are plenty of people who wouldn't mind. But I'm betting you're not a revolutionary. You'll think twice.'

Keeper paused. 'In the end, I'd make the same decision.'

'Then you would.'

'Don't leave it up to me,' Keeper insisted.

'Who, then? Don't expect anyone in the family to operate. Or the twins themselves – they'll never look in the mirror and see a monster.'

The responsibility was massive. Did Holman really care about the impartial opinion? Or did he need to unshoulder the decision out of weakness? No, thought Keeper, it was hardly weak to be going against the basic bureaucratic instinct for self-preservation. But Holman obviously had his limits. A particular constellation of events made this the time and place that the circle of obedience could be breached. But if Keeper didn't help Holman out of it now, the circle would close and keep him its unwilling prisoner.

'How would you get information to me?' Keeper asked.

'Where are you going from here?'

Now Keeper knew. 'Paris. Before I can judge anything you pass along, I'll need to know if Roy really went for the book – or on a wild-goose chase rigged by the Russians.'

'Why?'

'If all the trouble was for Yolkin, I could believe he was worth your Siamese twins having an argument about whether to give him up or keep him. And the tough one settled the argument his way.'

Holman frowned and nodded. 'Any idea where you'll stay?'

'No.'

Holman pondered. 'When you get to Paris cable me an address. You'd be sending one anyway so I could forward the rest of Roy's things.'

Schub had handed over only a few small personal effects: Roy's watch, a pair of shoelaces, some Turkish coins, and a postcard of the Blue Mosque. The postcard was addressed to Susan, and in the message space Roy had written, 'Hi! Dig it here. Love.' It still needed a stamp. The rest of Roy's baggage was reportedly in a hotel in some Turkish fishing village. Holman would have it retrieved by consular staff in Turkey.

'Give me an address other than a hotel,' Holman added. 'We don't want too many people poking around in your mail.'

'Can't we get around the mails?' Keeper asked. 'If what you have to send me is out of some secret file –'

'We don't have any tricks up our sleeve,' Holman replied. 'We're just amateurs.'

Keeper smiled. He was picking up right where Roy had left off. 'How about Roy's address?' he suggested.

'That would seem natural,' Holman agreed. 'I will try to find some obscure way of passing things to you, anyway. I have a friend on the Paris staff; he might help out, if he thinks he's doing a harmless personal favour.' He paused, plainly burdened by the thought of deceiving a friend. 'One way or another, expect to receive something very soon or not at all. I can't do any sustained snooping without giving myself away. And the odds are that, if anything damning does exist in tangible form, it won't be left lying around the Embassy for very long.'

'So the sooner you get started, the better,' Keeper observed.

'I'll have to finish my duties here first. You want the body sent to Paris?' Keeper thought, then nodded. 'There's apt to be a problem.'

'Schub said he'd co-operate.'

'Even so,' Holman sighed, 'there's always red tape.'

'How long will it take?'

'Anybody's guess.'

There was a silence.

'About our deal,' Holman said finally. 'You know, don't you – you know what you've agreed to? I mean, the penalty if you're caught receiving secret papers from me ...'

'I know,' Keeper said. 'I've thought about that already.'

Holman straightened the glass shakers, brushed the spilled black and white specks off the tablecloth. 'I guess we ought to be settling up, then,' he said, and waved to a waiter.

When Holman asked for the bill the waiter unloosed a babble of Russian and gesticulated grandly towards Stringbean and the fat man. The Russians rose and smiled, both making modest little bows.

'*Spaseebo*.' Holman smiled at them politely. 'Guess what, Keeper?'

'I see.' Keeper pushed back his chair and stood. 'More of that famous Russian hospitality.'

Panneau Frères

It was brilliantly sunny, but cold. The grey Parisian winter would be settling in soon. Dead brown leaves hopped across the courtyard on gusts of wind like so many horned toads. Keeper heard the scratch of their crisp edges against the flagstones.

He had chosen the small Left Bank hotel rather than one of the larger luxury hotels so that he would be able to move about freely. Here there was little chance of being recognized by some business acquaintance or news correspondent. Holman had assisted the plan by delaying his report on Keeper's travel arrangements so it would reach the Paris embassy too late for Keeper to be met at the airport. The late arrival of a telegram could always be blamed on Russian interference with communications. Keeper would have to come forward to claim the body when it arrived. But until then his personal investigation would be unhampered by the crush of news gatherers, or by stealthy surveillance.

That had been the plan. But as Keeper looked down into the courtyard he wondered if it had been naïve. At other times of the year it was undoubtedly pleasant to have breakfast at one of the glass-topped wrought-iron tables spotted around the central fountain. But for the man who was sitting there now it could not be so pleasant. The day was sunny, but cold.

And was it only imagined that, as the man sipped his coffee, his glance went frequently to Keeper's window? Keeper rubbed his eyes and stretched his arms high until the bones in his elbows and shoulders cracked. He had risen after a long deep sleep, so deep perhaps that in the first few moments of waking distinctions between memory and reality, past and present, were blurred. Perhaps he was superimposing the sensations of yesterday – looking from that hotel window in Batumi, feeling him self constantly watched – onto this morning. A man was having breakfast outside on a sunny day. There was nothing more to it.

He left the window and dressed. As he was about to leave the room, a porter knocked on the door and handed in a tray with coffee and croissants. A folded French newspaper was also on the tray. Looking at the front page while he drank his coffee, Keeper saw Roy's name in a headline; and there was a picture of a hawk-faced man with unruly grey hair captioned 'Semyon Lyndoushkine'.

After breakfast, Keeper set out to find a bookstore. It was Lyndushkin's Parisian publisher, according to Culdiev, who had made arrangements for smuggling out the manuscript. Culdiev hadn't given the publisher's name, but it would be printed on the binding of Lyndushkin's earlier books.

He came to a bookstore in the same street as the hotel. But neither *Le Diable des Pommes de Terre* nor *L'orchestre* could be found on the shelves. The salesgirl was sorry; the small supply had sold out, there had been so much demand for the two books in the past few days.

Because the Sorbonne was nearby, there were numerous booksellers carrying the work of distinguished Russian dissident authors. Keeper stopped into seven stores before finally locating a copy of *L'orchestre*. Stamped on the binding was the publisher's name: Panneau Frères. Keeper noticed many other contemporary Russian works bearing the same imprint.

At an office of the Poste-Téléphone-Télégraphe, he found the publisher's address in a directory. There was no listing for Roy – the phone book seemed to be several years old – so he cabled Holman to send 'personal effects' to the *poste restante* of this office.

Then he took a taxi to the address given for Panneau Frères.

It was in St Cloud, on a street shared with only a few other large residences. Turning through tall iron gates, the taxi travelled a long curving driveway around a small park, beautifully manicured flat lawns on which several peacocks were strutting. The drive led up to a scaled-down jewel-box chateau.

Keeper waited until the taxi had driven out to the street

before pushing the gold button beside the entrance. A call of chimes was answered by a girl dressed in assembly-line chic, a pencil lodged behind her ear so that the point poked out of her long brown hair. Through the open door, Keeper heard the busy chatter of typewriters, the ring of a telephone quickly answered.

'*Oui?*'

'My name is Keeper . . .'

The girl's hand fluttered to the pencil and removed it. What was it, this sudden neatening – a signal of respect? No, there was something else in the girl's stricken blue eyes. Fear? Shame? Keeper couldn't make it out. But it was certain from the quickness and intensity of her reaction that Roy's connection with the business wasn't a holy secret; even a secretary knew.

'*S'il vous plaît.*' The girl stepped back and gestured Keeper inside. Closing the door, she pointed off the entrance hall into a waiting room at the left, then went quickly away up a stairway to a second-floor balcony.

One wing of the house had been adapted to a suite of offices. A man was sitting in the waiting room turning the pages of a magazine. Beyond, through open doors, Keeper saw secretaries at desks typing, a man talking on the phone with his feet propped up on a stack of new books. He did not go into the waiting room, but loitered in the hall scanning the cases set into the walls which displayed the firm's recent publications. A cookbook, a biography of Berlioz, a thin volume of poems, and a huge volume of butterfly photographs occupied one case. In another, the books were all by authors with Slavic names, or dealt with subjects related to Communist history: a biography of Lenin, a study of Russian diplomatic relations with the Nazis, a post-mortem of the 1968 invasion of Czechoslovakia. When he had finished perusing the displays, Keeper glanced idly towards the balcony. The girl was there, staring down. He had the impression that she had been watching him for several seconds. Her hands were gripping the balustrade so tightly the knuckles were white.

'Would you come, please,' she said quickly. 'Monsieur le Comte Panneau is waiting.'

She met him at the top step and showed him to the middle door of three lining the balcony.

Keeper entered a long high-ceilinged room. At one end a harpsichord and a large antique globe occupied the corners; on the wall were subtly illuminated shelves filled with small carved ivory figurines and porcelain miniatures; several silk-upholstered chairs and a settee were grouped at the centre of this area. The far end of the room was a work place furnished with a desk, a conference table, and a wall of cork tiles to which was tacked a profusion of memos, illustrations, and mock-ups for dust jackets.

As Keeper entered, a man rose from behind the desk. He was tall and narrowly built, with full snow-white hair swept back in a leonine pompadour, and a sun-lamp tan. Keeper put his age at something over fifty; each year since had been surrendered grudgingly. A youthful aspect was carefully accentuated in the effete informality of his clothes, velvet slacks and a billowy white satin shirt open at the neck. Displaying white even teeth in an exaggerated smile, he moved forward with the studied languidity of one used to having people wait on his words. His pinched straight nose and small, slightly prissy mouth combined to give his face a look of permanent disdain.

'Comte Lucien Panneau,' he announced, extending a welcoming hand. As Keeper took it, he added sombrely, 'Allow me to offer my deepest sympathies.'

'If it makes you feel better.'

Panneau gave Keeper a careful look, then turned to the girl, who was still in the doorway. 'That will be all, Celine.' When the door had clicked shut, he turned back to Keeper and motioned him towards the settee. 'Please ... may I give you some coffee?'

'No.'

'You prefer a drink?'

'Nothing.' Keeper sat down on the settee.

The Frenchman shrugged and crossed the room to a table behind his desk. An electric percolator and cups were set out on the table. He poured himself some coffee, then came and sat opposite Keeper.

'It is easy to see you come in a bitter frame of mind, Mr

Keeper. Mere words, small kindnesses, you will have none of them. Perhaps your only comfort would be in knowing that others suffer, too. Your son's death will trouble me for the rest of my life.'

'I'm glad to hear that,' Keeper said. 'After the way it ended, I thought you might deny even knowing him.'

Panneau bristled. 'Mr Keeper, you would not be here if reliable informants had not revealed my connection. You know, therefore, I was trying to do something worthwhile. I have no wish to decline responsibility for that.'

'And who takes responsibility for his death?'

'You may accuse me of lack of perception, failing to detect his instability. But in the way he died, the responsibility could be none but his own.'

'Roy didn't kill himself,' Keeper said shortly. 'He was murdered.'

After a moment, Panneau shook his head. 'No. This is absurd. The news said he was being exchanged. It is not rational to make such arrangements one day, and destroy them the next.'

'You think it's more rational that he decided life wasn't worth living just as he was being set free?'

'Ah. There is the crux.' Panneau delicately set aside his coffee cup. 'Suicide is not a rational act. It happens quite often at unlikely moments, without any clear motive. Outwardly happy men leave the dinner table after a good meal to go and jump out the window. To say that your son was assassinated, however, there must be a motive. I see none.'

'I see several,' Keeper said curtly. 'I also see, from what I know of the details for smuggling out *The Mushroom Cave*, that you could have set Roy up to be caught.'

There were flashes in Panneau's cold grey eyes, chips of mica in stone. 'To whom have you talked? It seems they were not so reliable, after all.'

'Kiril Culdiev – are his references good enough? I spoke to him three days ago in Batumi.'

'Culdiev,' the Frenchman gasped. 'He accused me?'

'No. He was only worried that the network had been used by the KGB. It's my own idea that maybe you were more than a helpless pawn.'

Panneau laughed nervously. 'Do you know, Monsieur, that I was responsible for smuggling *L'orchestre*, Lyndushkin's last book?'

'I hear it was a good read, but pretty harmless. It would have been a cheap way of establishing credit with the samizdat people – so KGB could monitor what came out, stop anything really dangerous. Or else put the network to its own uses.'

For the first time, Panneau looked deeply troubled. 'You are terribly wrong. I swear –'

'Culdiev also said you'd arranged to send a trained agent for a secret landing.'

'*Merde!*' Panneau slapped his knees with both hands and sprang up. He faced out through the window for a few seconds then whirled on Keeper. 'I begin to wonder who has been used. You are told a story and, because of it, you come here in a mood to destroy my work. I know you have the means to do this; now I see you have the temperament. So the help I have given the samizdat network would be finished. Who would profit then, Monsieur? Think!' Softening his voice, he added, 'Can you say beyond a doubt that you spoke to the real Culdiev?'

'... an invalid ...' But Keeper knew even as he began to assemble the description that it was useless.

'An invalid!' Panneau snorted. 'Is there but one in all of Russia? Are there none who would co-operate to get special concessions, medical treatment? You could not have spoken to the real Kiril Culdiev. He would not have told you this story.'

'All right, Panneau,' Keeper said. 'I'll listen to yours.'

During the Frenchman's vigorous defence his long white hair had shaken loose over his eyes; he combed the hair away with his slender, bony fingers, taking a few more moments than necessary, preening.

At last he sat down again and began: 'A little less than two months ago I received a message informing me that the Lyndushkin manuscript was available but could not be sent out in the usual way. I did not question this. I understood there were reasons to take special precautions.'

'Who brought the message?' Keeper asked.

'As I see you are prone to confront people whose names are given to you, I will not reveal my contacts. I must preserve these confidants. However, it is the content of the message that should interest you, not the bearer. It included details of how the manuscript could be obtained. The plan was simple. On the afternoon of the seventeenth day of October, a small fishing trawler would cruise an area of the Black Sea parallel to the Russian-Turkish border, staying well within sight of land. I was to send a second boat to the same area with only one person on board. Provided that this person was dressed in a prescribed fashion and said an identifying phrase in English – something about "going to the library" as I recall – the manuscript would be handed over when the boats made a rendezvous.' The count gave a delicate smile, the sort of smile his ancestors would have used to deny court intrigues to the king's face. 'You must agree that no part of this plan called for the talents of special agents or green berets. There were no secret landings, no blowing up of fortresses ... but something sensible, uncomplicated, and as such things go, not unreasonably dangerous.'

'He was caught,' Keeper observed.

'I did not say there were absolutely *no* risks. But you may be sure your son understood them. He made us meet his price.'

'You paid him?'

'Of course,' Panneau replied. 'Fifteen thousand francs – almost three thousand dollars. My first offer was only twelve thousand.'

'Then that's why he took the job. But why did you offer it to him?'

'Mr Keeper, I was not auditioning actors for a film part. There were no lines outside my door. I asked the few people I know who might do this kind of thing – a couple of journalists, authors, a lawyer; those I thought had the time, the courage, and the motive. Some had the motive, but not the courage; others had the courage, but not the time. All my first attempts to find a courier failed. It was only when I found no one else that my secretary brought Roy to me.'

Keeper searched Panneau's face for the slightest hint of dissimulation. There was none. But the count belonged to a club that had retained its privileges across the centuries with cunning pitted against force of numbers. Perhaps that had bred in a talent for lying without conscience, without constraint.

160

'You expect me to believe you entrusted this job to a stranger,' said Keeper, 'on the recommendation of a stenographer?'

Panneau gazed unflinchingly at Keeper, then rose and crossed the room. Leaning over his desk, he barked a sharp order into the intercom. He straightened up then and stood staring at Keeper until there was a knock on the door.

'Entrez!' Panneau called crisply.

The girl came in. She looked paradoxically both more carefully composed and more unnerved than when Keeper had first seen her. It was as though, knowing she would be summoned to an account, she had spent the intervening time before a mirror making herself up; then, when the call had come, she had spoiled the veneer by anxiously running up the stairs. Aware now that she had known Roy, Keeper took a closer look. She was about twenty, fairly pretty. If she had been able to grow up in a pampered environment, had acquired the special grace of someone like Panneau, she might have been beautiful. But her life had evidently been tedious and sad; something had calloused her in a way that stole from her looks. There was a greyness about her face, and she was too thin, as though she dieted compulsively without regard to the proper shape of her body, which was full rather than fragile.

'Assieds-toi, Celine.'

She walked to a chair and sat down, her eyes averted. Panneau went and stood beside her.

'Celine, Mr Keeper is interested to learn how his son came to assist me. His questions are perhaps best answered by you. Would you mind?'

'Non, Monsieur le Comte.'

Panneau nodded to Keeper, but before he could begin, the girl looked up dolefully and said:

'It is because of me, if that is what you wish to know. I brought him into it.' She seemed relieved to accept the guilt.

'How and why?' said Keeper.

'Monsieur?'

'How long had you known him? Where did you meet?'

'He was attending some courses at La Sorbonne, French literature. A friend of mine was in one of these classes. She met him, they start to be lovers.' She made a thoughtful *moue*. 'So then I meet him. This was a few months ago.'

The timing was important. 'Exactly how many months?' Keeper asked.

The girl thought. 'Almost four. It was a party, just before Bastille Day.'

'And after that, did you see him often?'

She shrugged. 'He was living with my friend. When I saw her, I saw him.'

'So you were casual acquaintances.'

'With a girl friend's lover, it is wise to be no more.'

Keeper's tone hardened. 'Why would you trust this proposition to someone you didn't know very well?'

'I knew Monsieur le Comte needed someone –'

'But not just anyone,' Keeper broke in. 'Someone he could trust. What made you pick Roy?'

She hesitated. 'It was a thing of the moment. I know, perhaps it was not ...' She trailed off and looked down at her hands. They lay in her lap one over the other, presenting an outward appearance of calm. But Keeper could see the fingers of her upper hand were curved under, viced tightly between the fingers below. She started to speak again, her voice more emotional, unsteady. 'It is hard. I know but for me, he would be –'

Panneau interrupted, laying a hand on the girl's shoulder. 'I think it is too hard for you. I should not have asked.'

'No,' she cried suddenly. '*C'était juste*. I must account for myself.'

Slowly Panneau withdrew his restraining hand. The girl looked back to Keeper. There was no trace of the regret that had softened her features a moment earlier; she had denied it herself like a luxury she could not afford.

'It was, as I said, *prime-sautier* ... on an impulse. Even against my first intentions. When Monsieur le Comte had not found someone, he asked if I would suggest a friend. I said no. I did not want the responsibility to give so much danger. Then, one night, just two or three days after, I was with Roy and Jeanne. We had gone to the *cinéma*, one of those old American pictures that show often on *la rive gauche*, a Western with Errol Flynn. After, we walked a lot and Roy said nothing. It was clear

162

the movie had made him think about his home, how he could not go back. We came to St Germain. A crowd was there making a manifestation ... a *proteste*. During those days a revolutionary newspaper was being suppressed and the young *éditeurs* were on trial. This night the students had made a mob and many gendarmes came to stand against them. It was not yet bad when we arrived. The gendarmes stood on one side talking to each other; the students stood on the opposite; the tourists sat at Les Deux Magots watching it all over their drinks. It was like that ... until we came. The sight of it did something to Roy. There was an argument inside him, now it burst out. He pushed in front of the students and began to shout. To the police he shouted insults, to the students he shouted encouragement to act instead of staring like spectators at a sport. He wasn't even speaking French, but it set things off somehow. The students became bold and moved up behind Roy, began to shout with him. And then the gendarmes ...' Her eyes focused on some distant point, darting nervously, as if following the panic of colliding crowds. 'They swung their *matraques* like axes, cutting down anyone in the way. And Jeanne ... when they charged she tried running to Roy. They clubbed her, opened her head. We didn't know what to do then. Roy carried her out of it. He was coughing so from the gas it was a struggle not to drop her. He was too stunned to move; he just stood in a side street, her blood dripping on his shoes, until I pulled him away.' Her haunted eyes focused again on Keeper. 'We took her in a hospital and sat there until her parents came. Then we left. He wanted to talk, so I walked with him. All night I listened. He had such great guilt from everything, such confusion. He kept trying to act in a good way, and with each try it went against him – hurt the people he loved. He was so desperate to do something that would make them proud, that would not bring shame and doubt.' Her voice sank almost to a whisper. 'The next day I gave his name to Monsieur le Comte.'

Panneau moved around from behind her chair. 'The rest you know, Mr Keeper. I invited him here, gave him the details, and we agreed on a price.'

'Just like that,' Keeper said dubiously. 'He didn't need a day or two to think it over?'

'The concern was my need, not his. It was only a week before the rendezvous date; if he said no, I would have to find someone else. I had to demand a decision then and there.'

Keeper looked from Panneau to the girl and back to Panneau, as if expecting to catch them whispering a signal. 'Time, motive, courage,' he said, 'those were the three requirements, weren't they? Roy had the time. But the motive isn't clear. You say he came here and haggled over the price, that the motive was money.' He turned again to the girl. 'And you say it was conscience, ideals.'

'I do not contradict,' she said. 'He needed the money. But first came the needs of his soul.'

Keeper nodded equivocally. 'That still leaves "courage". Roy was a real long shot on that, wasn't he? He was only living over here because he was running away.'

'Stupid,' the girl muttered. 'You are so stupid. You think because he would not fight your war he was a coward? We fought your same insane war long before you, monsieur. They were the cowards who listened to the generals, who went off to die for nothing. Roy was brave. If only more ...'

She broke off, looking suddenly like a sleepwalker coming awake in the middle of a highway, wide-eyed and confused. Without finishing her thought, she turned to stare out the window.

Panneau regarded her sympathetically.

'Celine's father was a major in the Army,' he said finally to Keeper. 'He was killed at Dienbienphu.'

The girl stood up. 'May I go now?'

Panneau nodded and went to open the door for her. Just before she passed through, she paused, her back to the room. There was something else she wanted to say, Keeper thought. But it was only a small hesitation, and she went without another word. Panneau remained standing at the open door.

'We have told you all we can,' he said stiffly.

'Not quite all.' Keeper rose and walked towards Panneau. 'Culdiev said messages between you took weeks to go back and forth ...'

'That is true.'

'It makes sense,' Keeper said, 'assuming you had to rely on a loose system of contacts – that the messages didn't go by radio, or travel with priorities. And yet you said Roy turned up for the job only a week before the rendezvous. So that would be two or three weeks after you had to send a message telling Culdiev that someone was coming for the book.' He stopped directly in front of Panneau. 'Either you knew Roy for more than a week, or you had a fast way of transmitting messages.'

'Neither is the case,' Panneau replied. 'I did agree to the rendezvous long before meeting Roy. I did not want to lose a chance at the book, so I had to bet I would find someone. In the end, if there had been no one else . . .' He drew himself up slightly, a patrician expression of modest pride.

'You would have gone?'

Panneau nodded. 'But one does not send an old man to do a boy's job if it can be avoided. The trip, the sailing, it would have been rigorous. Better to delegate . . .'

Keeper hesitated.

'Something else?' Panneau asked.

'No,' Keeper muttered. 'Not now.'

He was halfway down the stairs when Panneau called to him. 'Mr Keeper, I wish now I had made the journey.' Keeper didn't look back. As he reached the bottom step he heard the door of Panneau's office close quietly.

He expected someone to show him out, but the foyer was empty. Glancing beyond the waiting room, he saw Celine alone in an office, sitting at a desk, head down in her hands, the long brown hair hanging over her face. He remembered then there was something he wanted from her.

She didn't look up when he came into the office.

'Can you give me Roy's address?' Keeper asked.

She took a piece of paper and wrote, bending over it intently like a child doing an exercise.

'Does the girl still live there?'

She shook her head.

'Then put down where I can find her.'

She wrote another line dutifully. Handing him the paper, she raised her face enough so that Keeper saw she was crying. Hurriedly she lowered her head again and plucked some paper handkerchiefs from an open drawer.

He had no impulse to console her.

Once outside the house, Keeper looked at the piece of paper, read the two addresses: ROY, 25 RUE JACOB JEANNE FERRÉ, HÔPITAL LAENNEC, 42 RUE DE SÈVRES, 7ᵉ. Roy's girl was still in the hospital; she must have been hurt seriously. But so badly that Roy had sought to compensate by hurling himself blindly into danger, by taking his own life?

Keeper had just turned through the gates into the street when he heard a chilling scream behind him. He spun around, to discover it was the cry of a peacock. The bird's neck was craned upward, the hideous cry rising from its blue-black throat. The beautiful tail was fully fanned out. It looked, Keeper thought, like a domed hedge through which dozens of bright blue eyes were covertly peeking, spying on him.

Black and White

The nurse at the reception desk regarded Keeper blankly until he showed her the piece of paper.

'Ah. Jeanne Ferré.' She started to explain something in rapid French, but cut herself off and picked up the phone. After a short conversation she hung up. '*Attendez*,' she said crisply, and returned to jotting entries in a ledger.

Keeper took a chair in a nearby waiting area. A second nurse, built like a masseuse and wearing steel-rimmed spectacles, marched up to him a minute later. He rose and looked at her inquiringly.

'You come to see Jeanne Ferré?' she said.

Keeper nodded.

'I'm sorry, monsieur. She cannot speak to you.'

'For a minute –'

'It is not a question of time,' the nurse said impatiently. 'She can speak to no one. She is still in a coma.'

Keeper paused. 'How long has she been unconscious?'

'Since the night they brought her.'

'When was that?'

Weary of Keeper's questions, the nurse made a cross tight mouth; but she answered one more. 'Two weeks.'

'Could I . . . just look at her?' It was becoming a reflex. He could trust nothing, believe nothing unconfirmed by his senses. Could the girl really not speak to him? Was she only an incidental victim?

The nurse inspected him curiously. 'You are not a friend?'

'No.'

She shook her head. 'If you are not a friend, or of the family –'

'It was my son who brought her here,' Keeper said. 'They lived together.'

The nurse raised her eyebrows, then nodded slowly. 'You may see, but not go in. A minute, no more.' Turning stiffly, she motioned him to follow with a slight snappish gesture of her hand, as though to a small dog.

An elevator took them to the fifth floor, where the nurse led the way through double doors over which the sign read 'NEUROLOGIQUE'. Halfway along the corridor, she pointed through the glass window of a door.

He could see very little of the girl. She was swathed in sheets below her neck, bandages above. Like trees bearing glass fruit, metal poles hung with bottles surrounded the bed, feeding fluids into her body. A wavy line of light blipped across the screen of an electronic instrument at one side of the bed. On the other side by a window an elegantly dressed middle-aged woman flipped through the pages of a magazine automatically, as if her own scanning mechanism were synchronized with the electronic heartbeat. Suddenly she glanced up and caught Keeper at the window.

He recoiled, feeling that he had seen an accusation in the woman's glance. It was a foolish feeling, he knew. Yet it lingered for quite a while after he had left the hospital, a lurking sense that the suffering of innocents had begun not with Roy's decision, but some choice of his own.

Twenty-five Rue Jacob was an old building of five storeys, neither cheap nor showy, situated on a street of inexpensive hotels and expensive little shops. Roy's name appeared beside the top button on an illuminated roster. As the sun did not penetrate into the doorway, much less into the narrow street, the light was helpful. Keeper pressed the bottom button labelled 'CONCIERGE'. He rang six times before a spindly woman with short frizzy red hair answered the door. Above her wrinkled face the roots of her red hair showed stark white.

He told her his name.

'Keeper? *Il est mort.*'

'I'm his father,' Keeper explained.

She looked at him flintily without a flicker of comprehension and started to close the door.

He bolstered his shoulder against it and repeated his name,

thumping a hand on his chest. But the concierge struggled against him until he took a five-dollar bill from his pocket and thrust it at her. She released her hold on the door to take the money. As though the cash was a genealogy on which she could read the family link, she turned the bill in her hands for a second and burst out, '*Il était votre fils*, the child ...' Then she hurried away down a dark hall to an apartment at the rear, and returned with a key. There was no elevator in the building. Handing over the key, the concierge pointed to the stairs and left Keeper to climb them alone.

Immediately on entering the apartment he was struck by an eerie sensation. As in tales where deserted ships are found at sea, not a soul on board and yet the engines throbbing, meals cooking in the galley and cards dealt on the table, Keeper had the feeling that life had been interrupted here only recently, a day ago, less. But Jeanne had been in the hospital for weeks; Roy had been captured more than a week ago, had left Paris days before that. Perhaps it was an illusion of the sort achieved in museum displays which flawlessly re-create historic rooms; a cover left off an inkwell, a drawer left ajar, urged some expectation of living presences. It was like that here. Everything had been set down or thrown down as if soon to be picked up again. Books and records were scattered over shelves and furniture; clothes, too. Keeper saw a pair of nylon stockings balled up on a chair, a pair of high-heeled shoes askew under a glass-topped coffee table, a skirt crumpled in a ring on the floor, as if it had been stepped out of where it lay.

Despite the disorder, the apartment appealed to him. Unlike the overworked schemes of decorators his wives had employed, this was slapdash and relaxed. Mixed with the plain modern furniture were oddities: an antique slot machine, a hooded wicker chair that hung by a chain from the ceiling.

He walked along the hall leading off the living room and came to a small kitchen. The sink was full of dirty dishes. Used pans, some with food still in them, stood atop the stove. And in a straw basket on a counter there were some oranges and a bunch of bananas. The bananas were bright yellow, some even slightly green. Keeper opened the refrigerator. Two bottles of milk, butter in a dish, a few tomatoes, and a small steak wrapped in brown paper were distributed over the shelves. He picked up the steak and smelled it, then the milk. They were fresh.

At the end of the hall was a bedroom. A bed, a wardrobe, and a dresser. Propped unframed beside the mirror of the dresser was a photograph of Roy posing intimately with a girl in a bikini on a sunny strand of empty beach. Keeper held the photograph up to the light through the window. A breeze from the sea had partially obscured the girl's face with wind-blown hair. But he was almost positive the girl was Panneau's secretary.

He looked through the dresser drawers for other clues. Nothing turned up until he went back to the living room. There on a shelf by the telephone, Keeper found a collection of odd household papers – bills, receipts, old telephone messages, and a chequebook printed with Roy's name from the Paris branch of an American bank. A deposit of $2,800 had been noted on the next-to-last cheque stub, dated October 11. That much of Panneau's story must be true: Roy had been paid, and he had received the money only a week before the date of the rendez-vous.

The phone rang as Keeper was thumbing through the chequebook. He answered. 'Hello.'

'*Allo, Maman? Celine.*'

He understood nothing she said after that. She rattled on in French. There was no pause at the end, no chance for Keeper to speak. She said '*Au revoir,*' and the phone clicked, dead.

At twilight she came, letting herself in with a key. She was carrying a large red-striped paper bag printed with the name of a store. When she saw Keeper swinging in the suspended wicker chair, she came and stood before him, as if presenting herself to be judged.

'I loved him,' she said softly, hopelessly. Then she turned and glanced distractedly around the apartment. 'Such a mess,' she mumbled. 'But I have been sleepwalking.' She put the bag on the table and started to gather the scattered clothing.

Keeper watched silently.

'Why did you lie?' he asked finally.

'I wish for Panneau to go on trusting me,' she said wearily. 'He would not if he knows I cared. He will realize I am there now to watch, to take some proof . . .' Her mouth arched down in a bitter pout.

'Proof of what?'

She said nothing, but nodded at the gaily coloured shopping bag. Then she carried the bundle of dirty clothes out of the room.

Keeper went to the bag and rummaged inside. On top, as if swiped by a compulsive shoplifter, was an indiscriminate collection of scarves and lingerie. This had seemingly been dumped in to conceal what lay at the bottom, a package the size and thickness of a small briefcase, brown paper tied up with string. He lifted out the package. It weighed several pounds. Pulling away the string and wrapping, he found a stack of torn, crumbling pages.

He carried the papers to the sofa, sat down, and picked through them. There were four or five hundred pages, he thought; no way to be certain, some were numbered, some weren't. The size and quality of the paper was not uniform. Ten or twenty pages in sequence would be of good quality bond; then there would be a section of tissue, or coarse wrapping scissored down to size. On some the writing had been done in ink, on others in pencil, a few were typed; one short section was in black crayon.

Keeper could read none of it. The script was Cyrillic, visibly set down by the same hand, although in later sections it became progressively shakier and less controlled. The writing had apparently been done in snatches over a long period, the materials cadged from constantly changing sources.

He looked up from the manuscript to find Celine leaning in the hall doorway, still wearing her trench coat, her hands shoved down in the pockets.

'The book,' she said, '*The Mushroom Cave.*'

He had known. But how . . . ?

'Panneau had it?' asked Keeper.

'Not this morning, not when you were there. Perhaps then he did not even know it was coming.' She eked out a smile, thin, ironic. 'He said I should pretend to steal it for you. Since you would find out soon enough it had come through. But this way you might do something with it yourself, give it to the press. A better publicity, you see?'

'How did he get it?'

'It was brought this afternoon.' She heaved her shoulders. 'Perhaps it was always in the plan. This is what I suspect after Roy was killed. They are too careful not to have known ...' With a hollow look at Keeper, she added, 'But I would not have agreed, if I had ...' She trailed off.

'What was the true beginning? How did Roy get pulled in?'

'There are so many beginnings. My reasons, his, theirs.' She shivered. 'I will take a drink. You?'

Keeper shrugged.

She went out to the kitchen. There was a clinking of ice cubes, but she did not reappear for several minutes. When she did she had removed her trench coat and changed out of her office clothes. She was barefoot, wrapped in an orange terry-cloth kimono. In each hand was a tumbler of ice and whisky, more than just a sociable amount. She handed Keeper a glass.

'We had only Bourbon. Roy liked it.'

Keeper himself had always preferred Bourbon.

She sank down at the opposite end of the sofa and took a long pull from her drink. Then she said:

'For me the beginning was three years ago. I was hired then by Panneau. It did not take long to guess he had some sort of special affiliations. The business has never done very well since Panneau's brother died, in 1963. Gerard. He was the founder, the clever one. Lucien is not a good businessman, and the actual sales of his publications never came near to the amounts I would see listed on the accounts as foreign royalties. Not even sales of Lyndushkin's work, for all the *éclat*, were always good. So there was a mystery about this big income from abroad. But it did not trouble me. Panneau paid always very well, with good raises. And I was never asked to make anything but the normal work of a private secretary. Until three months ago.'

'When Roy came into it,' Keeper put in.

'*Oui.* Panneau called me to his office one morning. He said someone was needed to carry out a mission – the one he described to you; just that, the details were the same. He explained, too, what was the prize, the importance, everything. Then he asked my help in getting someone to do the job. This was Roy. I was to make the approach, interest him in the proposition, make payment –'

'You mean Roy had already been picked out? Without his knowing ...?'

'*Exactement.*'

'But why him?' Keeper asked.

'I never asked. Roy was only a name to me then. And Panneau promised a very good bonus for my help, *deux mille francs*; so I agreed with no questions. A week later, a man I had never seen before took me in a car from work. We parked outside La Sorbonne. When Roy emerged in a crowd of students, the man pointed him out.'

'He was from the group that controls Panneau?' Keeper asked.

'I assume. He is *Américain*; and it was he who came today, to bring Panneau the book.'

Keeper saw where she was leading him, saw himself at another crossroad in the maze.

'An American? Then Panneau has been working for us?' Us. What force of habit made him say it, including himself with those who might have doomed his son?

Celine looked at Keeper as if uncertain he had been listening. '*Et alors*, it is known the CIA take an interest in publishing. Your own newspapers have printed this. They are always mentioned when the more sensational books come out.'

Keeper thought of Parritt's calm denials, the all-American innocence.

'Did you ever get his name – the man who fingered Roy?'

'Today, he announced himself,' Celine said. But she had to struggle to remember. 'It was a word, something in English ... What is the talking bird?'

'Parritt?'

'*Oui.*'

So he had overseen the operation. Every step. 'All right. Go on. After he pointed Roy out to you ...'

She drank some more Bourbon. 'I got out of the car and followed. It was summer, a beautiful day. Roy walked to the Jardin

173

du Luxembourg and sat down to read a book. I sat near, we started to talk.' Her fingers drew convoluted trails through the frost on her glass. 'It was easy to meet, because we were attracted to each other. But that made the rest more difficult. I was afraid to tell Roy about the book. He would realize our meeting had been for a purpose, and he would despise me. Five days after we met, we started living together. With each day it was harder to tell him, to risk losing him.'

But it was she who had enlisted Roy, after all, Keeper reminded himself. Could he believe her now, any more than he had once believed Parritt?

'Or perhaps you merely delayed the proposition,' Keeper tested. 'Until you could soften him up.'

Anger sparked in her eyes. But the spark died almost instantly, the last belated sputter from a dry wick. Grief had filled every place inside her that might have harboured hate or anger. Her eyelids closed and tears seeped between the lashes.

'I cannot blame you for the idea, monsieur. But it was not that way.'

'Panneau was counting on Roy, wasn't he? He obviously expected you to do whatever was necessary.'

Celine shook her head. The tears dripped onto her cheeks. 'I did not need to play the prostitute in order to convince Roy. Panneau knew that.'

'How could he?'

'Your son had guilts,' Celine cried, 'that is the truth. Perhaps even such things can be recorded in a dossier, analysed by experts. Panneau knew that Roy had run from one obligation, saw that he might take this chance to redeem himself. There was the money, too, a good sum ...'

She had suddenly become more defensive, Keeper noticed; even physically, drawing her bare legs up so she was curled into a corner of the sofa.

'But Panneau wasn't displeased,' Keeper persisted, 'when he found out you were living with Roy.'

'He never found out. To this day he has no idea Roy and I were lovers. If I had told him he would have thought like you — that it was cheap, to earn the bonus.'

'You did earn it in the end,' Keeper observed.

'Yes,' Celine said pathetically, 'I did. But why do you say it so cruelly? I am hiding nothing now.'

'I'm sorry,' Keeper said. And afterwards he realized it was so.

Celine finished her drink. 'When I saw we might make a whole life together, I had to tell him anyway; not to persuade, but so our foundation would not be in deception. I kept putting it off, though.' She rubbed one hand back and forth over her forehead as though trying to remove a smudge. 'Then the riot happened. Jeanne was a friend of Roy's from La Sorbonne. That night she asked us to join the protest; she was in a Maoist group – there are many at the Université – and this was one of their causes. Roy refused. He pretended not to be interested in such things. On the way home, though, we passed St Germain; the rest was as I told you. Afterwards' – her voice sank to a whisper – 'I confessed to him.'

'Everything?' Keeper asked quietly.

Celine looked at him uncertainly.

'Did you tell Roy whose payroll he was really going on?'

'I told my suspicions,' she said. 'But it made no difference to him. He decided it was worth doing. And he did not blame me for having a part in it.' Some of the pain left her face. 'Please remember that. The final decision was always his. And he believed it was a good thing.'

'If only he'd known what we do,' Keeper said with sudden ferocity. 'He wouldn't have been so anxious to go, not at any price.'

Celine looked to her glass for relief, but it was empty.

'What did you mean,' Keeper asked, 'about watching Panneau to get proof?'

She kept a guilty silence.

Keeper set down his drink. 'It's the only way it makes sense, isn't it? That they knew Roy might be caught, even before he went; wanted it to happen. Lyndushkin's book was supposed to be coming out through the samizdat network, but it would be hard to keep the secret. With samizdats going through a pipeline of dedicated amateurs, the KGB was bound to pick up some whispers. They had to be given a good strong scent to follow, a dumb wooden duck to pounce on while the real bird flew. So Roy was sent. The Russians probably silenced him because they thought he really knew where the manuscript was hidden. But the murderers were on both sides, really. Panneau helped to kill him, and Parritt; they let him go, knowing what he was in for.'

'And I . . .,' Celine said miserably. 'I helped, too.'

Keeper picked up the manuscript. 'For this,' he muttered. He stared at the papers, the scrawled words. Words to kill. Now after everything else they had sent Celine to him, thinking he'd serve as the last link. And was there a choice? Without it the whole sickening business had no meaning. Roy would still be dead, and for nothing. Perhaps the manuscript had to be yielded up, even if it gave the murderers their alibi.

Alibis. Susan. What about her?

He saw now where she might have been drawn in. Roy had thought of the mission as a chance to recoup lost pride. He could have written her about it, included what Celine had told him about Panneau, the source of his funds. If Susan knew she might have threatened interference . . .

But it was a book, only a book! Could they play so callously. for nothing more? Eliminate her mindlessly as flicking some grit out of a clockwork? Why not? Parritt had minced no words about the underlying philosophy. It was a war, a battle for objectives. So pins were stuck in the maps, and orders dispatched. People didn't show on the maps, just pins. While the strategists worked for the good of humanity, lives got crowded off the planning board by coffee cups.

His fingers clenched around the manuscript like a living thing to be strangled for revenge. Would any lives be saved if it were printed? Surely more people would suffer. Did it matter who? Ours or theirs?

He viced both hands along one edge of the paper and moved them apart, trying to tear the whole thickness. It was too much. He let some of the loose pages slide to the floor, and kept ripping at the rest with quick wrenching jerks. But the paper resisted. Separately the pages could be destroyed so easily – like separate lives; formed together into a mass they withstood the stresses.

He relaxed his grip. All the pages fell away.

Celine had watched impassively.

'It wouldn't have mattered,' she said. 'They will have copies, photographs. It will be released even without you.'

Keeper stared at the paper littered around his feet. Celine put her head back and closed her eyes.

'What sort of proof can you get?' Keeper said finally.

'The accounts, some correspondence. It will not prove how they wasted Roy, but it will show Panneau is a tool. The newspapers here will be interested to know how the CIA perverts our print. Here at least Panneau will be finished.'

Keeper hauled himself to his feet. That wouldn't do for him, he thought, he would need a more even settlement of the bill. He went towards the door. Celine didn't lift her head or open her eyes.

Just before closing the door behind him, Keeper stopped.

'Will it make any difference to you where Roy is buried?'

She took a long moment to answer.

'Non.'

Reason

A block of lights burned in one section of the house, the wing given over to Panneau's office staff. As he walked up the drive, through the french windows Keeper saw a number of people moving slowly around on their feet, in regular patterns as in some eerily slow square dance. They were each holding a pile of paper, laying the sheets down one at a time as they moved.

The door chimes pealed and died. A minute passed. Then Panneau was there staring out, haggard, his age showing. He was dressed less foppishly now in a black polo-neck sweater and grey pants. One of his hands trembled very close by a pocket. There was an angular bulge in the pocket, Keeper noticed, and it sagged heavily.

'I thought it might be you,' Panneau said unhappily. He took a quick step backward, made no effort to stop Keeper from entering.

'It's Parritt I want,' Keeper said. 'Where is he?'

Panneau hesitated, then gestured to the closed doors of his office wing. 'In there. But, Keeper, you have the book. Let that be an ending. You will only hurt yourself otherwise.'

'You're worried about me?' Keeper sneered.

'Keeper . . . believe . . .' Panneau's hands groped the air, like an opera singer performing an aria. 'I didn't understand what they were doing . . .'

Keeper brushed past Panneau and thrust open the doors to the office wing.

Startled by Keeper's sudden entrance, the small group of men and women in the outer office froze. He recognized a few of them: secretaries he had seen on his earlier visit, the man who had been having coffee outside at his hotel this morning. They paused long enough to absorb the shock of his bursting in. But they seemed to be prepared for such an eventuality, and fell again into the moving pattern, distributing the pages in their hands onto the piles of paper set out on every available surface – desktops, chairs, even the carpets except where intersticing pathways had been left.

Keeper went to a side table and looked at the top page of one pile. It was mimeographed in French, but he could tell it was some sort of handout, a press release perhaps. The capitalized heading included Lyndushkin's name, and the short paragraph below started with tomorrow's dateline: PARIS, 30 Oct. The adjacent pile seemed to be the same story in German. At the other end of the table, Keeper found the English version.

MISSING WORK BY SEMYON LYNDUSHKIN COMES WEST
PARIS, Oct 30 – Panneau Frères, the French publishing house that has been instrumental in saving the work of many dissident Russian authors from extinction behind the Iron Curtain, announced today that it would publish *The Mushroom Cave*, Lyndushkin's autobiographical account of his service with the Soviet secret police from 1920 to 1937. The announcement is certain to have far-reaching effects in diplomatic as well as literary circles. It was on charges stemming from an alleged attempt to smuggle this book out of the U.S.S.R. that the Russians recently arrested Roy Keeper, a young American. Mr Keeper's subsequent death while in captivity was reported as 'suicide'.

Even a well-placed apostrophe, Keeper reflected, had its propaganda quotient. He read on. 'As the time period covered by the book coincides with Stalin's brutal purges ...' He had been told all of this.

Keeper moved along, scanning the piles. More pages of short paragraphs in different languages, different aspects of the news analysed. 'A NEW PHASE IN ESCALATING SOVIET CENSORSHIP.' 'THE LYNDUSHKIN MYTH.'

He found the book – the opening pages of the English version – in neat ranks of separate pages atop one of the desks. In one corner was the title page. Keeper lifted the top sheet from the next stack and read:

I was born in 1920. I do not mean it was then that I emerged from my mother's womb; I mean it was then that I was born as the man who writes this book, a man who must confess in these pages that he is a cheat, a thief, a sadist, a murderer. There was hope once that

179

I would be something better. When I first decided to become a Bolshevik, on an August day in 1915, talking with a friend in a sunny meadow of the Valdai hills, I was filled with noble feelings, a love for my country and its people. For these reasons I joined in a struggle to free them. But the system we chose had too many secrets. Like a dark cave, its floor damp with spilled blood, it was not fit for growing things of beauty and nourishment; only mushrooms with the power to kill. We who lived there fed on this poison. It killed the good in each of us. And there are men now who lead us –

'You'll have plenty of chances to read that. Come in here.'

Parritt stood in shirtsleeves framed in the doorway of a small inner office.

Keeper put the page back on its proper pile and walked into the room.

Parritt sat down again behind a desk, put his leg up on one corner. The only light in the room came from a desk lamp. A crescent curve of shadow from the lamp's domed metal shade sliced across Parritt's face, leaving just the lower half clearly visible.

There were two other chairs. One faced the desk squarely, set back a few feet. In the other, by the french windows, Keeper saw that Parritt had dumped his jacket, and over the back had slung his shoulder holster. It would be a relief to take off that holster, Keeper knew. He recognized the gun in it, a heavy weapon, highly powered; he had carried one like it in the Pacific, a forty-five. To hold it was an experience of power, let alone to fire it. A child's dream of a gun. Parritt would have chosen no other, Keeper thought.

He remained standing, silent.

'Do you really want to know?' Parritt said. 'Because you won't like it, not the whole story. Not where it comes out that maybe you're to blame for killing him. Go while you can, Keeper. Turn that manuscript into some newspaper and let your son die a hero.'

'And his mother,' said Keeper, 'what goes on her tombstone?'

Parritt shook his head, almost pityingly. 'You're still blind, still don't care how much it could hurt. And you'll go on, trying to rake it all up.'

'Somebody has to cut you down, Parritt.'

Parritt unslung his leg from the desk, sat forward and stared at Keeper. His clean-cut collegiate face came into the light, the expression of a sophomore trying to comprehend a complex equation on a blackboard.

'Of course, you could kill me, too,' Keeper went on. 'But you've already got one phony accident to arrange. An automobile wreck, I suppose – as soon as she's reported back in Wyoming. "Mrs Keeper had been under considerable strain since ..." Something along those lines. How will you explain the coincidence if I go on top of that? The whole family.'

It was strange, Keeper thought; in death they would somehow be a family again, killed together by the same forces.

'You overestimate your importance,' Parritt said calmly. 'We don't have to worry about any stories you tell. We're going to publish that book, fix it to give Roy some of the credit. That's what people will believe.'

'Without authentication? You gave away the original.'

Parritt smiled. 'I think it's time you took delivery of your mail,' he said, gesturing to the chair by the window. 'There's a letter in my jacket, inside pocket. Holman tried getting it out in the diplomatic pouch.'

Keeper didn't move.

'What's the matter, Keeper? You're after answers. Well, Holman made a lot of good guesses from the information he stole. He was smart. Read what he has to say.'

'What did you do to him?' Keeper asked quickly.

'I guess you could say we killed him. With kindness. He'll never hold a sensitive position again. But he'll make an above-average third assistant in some backwater. He was happy to let it go at that. He knew he'd gotten in too deep.' Parritt nodded again at the jacket. 'Go ahead.'

'Just tell it,' Keeper said tiredly.

'You won't trust me.'

'I won't trust the letter. I know how it works now: any means to an end. Except the means don't exist to convince me an innocent kid had to be –'

'He wasn't innocent,' Parritt said sharply. 'He ran out on one chance to serve his country. We gave him another.'

'What a beautiful way to die,' Keeper muttered,

'He wasn't supposed to die. That was the last thing w
wanted.'

'What you wanted doesn't concern me. It's how you tried t
get it. Why couldn't you use your own tin men to keep th
appointments?'

'We needed someone with a certain kind of background.'

'Oh, you loved his background,' Keeper said savagely. 'Yo
did everything you could to hide it.'

'From some people, yes,' Parritt declared. 'Look, we wer
engineering a trade. Roy's record wouldn't have earned him an
sympathy with the folks at home, if they'd known it. On th
other hand, in other important places, where they'd take th
trouble to dig, he would have shown as the kind of man we'
never cut in on a security operation.'

It was the trade Parritt was talking about, Keeper suddenl
realized; the deal for the Russian, not the book. What was hi
name – Yolkin? Had that been the priority? To make the Rus
sians think they were forcing his return?

'Read Holman's letter,' Parritt urged again.

Keeper stood still, waited.

'All right.' Parritt shrugged. 'I'll tell you what's in it. On
thing he wrote about is the mood in Moscow right now; tha
was one indicator. It's been tense for the past few days. Mor
than the usual amount of frightened rumours are circulating. A
lot of respectable Russians are getting unexpectedly wakenec
in the middle of the night, taken away for interrogation. The
party hierarchy has suddenly undergone some reshuffling
There's even talk of a purge, thirties-style. Holman probabl
wouldn't have understood it all, except that he decided to tak
a closer look at Pavel Yolkin's biography. Secret, but not top
secret. He already knew the most important fact – had ever
told you. But it was seeing it fleshed out, and coupling it wit
the aftermath of Roy's murder, that made things click.

'Yolkin was born in China. His father was a Russian Army
captain, part of the garrison the Russians established in Peking
in 1900 after they'd gone in with an international force to crush
the Boxer Rebellion. The captain married a Chinese girl and in
1911 they had a son. Pavel lived the first twenty-six years of his

life in China. During that time he became a Communist. He was on the Long March with Mao in 1934. But then in 1937 his paternal side took over. He went back to Russia, where he's been ever since, working for the KGB. They took him in gladly, since his youthful contacts might be useful. But he never got very far. As time went on, the Russians weren't short of men who'd had more recent direct experience in China. There was free movement between the countries until five years ago.

'What the KGB took thirty years to find out was that Yolkin was still Chinese at heart. Oh, they'd watched him when he came over, but he'd proved himself clean. As far as they knew. So he had thirty-odd years of sending back information to the Chinese Communists. With four thousand years of history behind them, they'd been smart enough to anticipate a day when a man well-placed to spy on the Russians might come in handy. But Yolkin did more than spy, we know now; he nursed a conspiracy of Chicom sympathizers right within the ranks of the Soviet regime. There are still plenty of Russians who believe the true proletarian revolution has yet to be fought. Whichever of them joined Yolkin, they put together a remarkable organization. In thirty years there was never a leak. Until a few months ago – when Yolkin was away, under KGB orders to run a trade mission to the United States. Then the chain of confidences he'd painfully spent so much time building broke one link. A small one, but enough to finger him as the key man. The Russians have rarely had bigger trouble in their intelligence division, or found it out at a worse time. But they had a chance to blow the whole chain, if they could only get Yolkin home still thinking he was a live agent. Then they could keep him under surveillance while he made his rounds. The trouble was they couldn't just order him home. Because by then we had him. He'd been picked up in Albuquerque, meeting a computer systems expert who's logged time at half a dozen of our Southwest missile bases. You with me, Keeper?'

Keeper had drifted to the windows, turned his back on the room. 'I'm listening,' he said. But was he? He heard the words, had begun to sense the outlines of their meaning. And yet they made no impact on his mind or heart, moved his sympathies neither one way nor the other. Was there some pitch he alone was deaf to, a frequency within the message that would have quieted the fury for other men?

'The Russians' one hope,' Parritt continued, 'was that we'd agree to co-operate if they just picked up the hot line and told us about Yolkin. It wasn't such a wild card. They know what our preference will be if there's a war between Russia and China. Some of us might say "when" there's a war. Since the incidents on the Ussuri River three years ago – remember. Russian and Chinese troops killing each other for the right to control a tiny island in the middle of the river? – there's been a build-up of their armies all along the Sino-Soviet border. Right now it adds up to millions of men facing each other along a line of four thousand miles. Millions – shivering with the cold and the fear and the waiting. Neither side wants it to happen, but they may be too nervous to avoid it. And when the push comes to shove out there, Keeper, there's no doubt where we want the advantage. We may have started talking with the Chinks, but it'll take another twenty-five years to arrive at where we are now with the Russians.'

Behind him Keeper heard the twang of a spring in a metallic office chair. He guessed that Parritt had sat back again, relaxed with the knowledge that he had made his point.

'How the plan was going to work, you know all that. The Russians had been so eager to move, they let us write the scenario, use the censorship issue. We couldn't send in a real operator; Yolkin might have suspected, then, that the exchange was rigged. Panneau thought we were really after the book; Celine, too. But she knew one more thing – exactly who Panneau was working for. I see now where we were careless. Even so, as long as our real target seemed to be the book, it wouldn't have mattered. Except that two days before he left for Turkey, Roy sat down and wrote his mother; he thought she'd like to know he'd done a job for his country, after all. On receiving the letter, she proceeded to inquire about it – pretty calmly. We might've squeaked through anyway, stalled her off. But we'd forgotten the nature of the beast we'd gone to bed with. The KGB were in on this operation all the way. They knew she had at least the potential to upset the cart, and there was too much at stake. So they –'

Parritt faltered. When he continued, his delivery lacked for the first time its customary smoothness.

'You see what they did – blackmailed us into going to the end, covering for them. You can curse us for that, Keeper, curse the whole operation. But the proof that it was worth trying is in what happened when Yolkin's friends got a hint that he'd been blown. How they did, we don't know. Maybe they just guessed, or simply decided not to risk taking him back. Or maybe it was your nosing around that tipped someone, Keeper ... yours. Anyway Yolkin's friends dealt with it to their advantage. It took someone pretty high up to slip an order for Roy's release into the chain of command. Then, when he was on the plane, it took one in a detachment of twelve rank-and-file soldiers to cut his throat. So it appears that Yolkin has friends in high places and low. Maybe only a couple, maybe an army. In the process of killing Roy, they've thrown shadows on the Kremlin wall that should give us all nightmares. Unless the Russians can track down exactly who ordered Roy's release – and I'm betting they can't, not for certain – there will really be a purge. At the very least, twelve army guards will be executed for, say, "profiteering"; and a couple of Russian generals will die in "plane crashes".'

Parritt fidgeted in his chair, leaned over trying to see Keeper's face. 'You see why you have to let it alone? These things can't be dredged up, not for the public. There's so much confusion now ... on a mass level this wouldn't be seen in the right perspective.' Parritt paused, waiting for some response.

Keeper said nothing, did not turn from the window.

When Parritt spoke again the edge of arrogance had returned to his voice. 'Accept it, Keeper. The book will neutralize you up to a point. Beyond that, if you do force us, we'd neutralize in other ways. You'd be responsible . . .'

There was a long silence.

'And the book?' Keeper asked finally. He was still looking through the window. Outside it had begun to drizzle.

'What about it?' Parritt said.

'How did you get the samizdat network to deliver so conveniently?'

Parritt chuckled, 'There was only one way. We wrote it.'

'So it doesn't even exist.'

'It might,' Parritt said passively. 'When a rumour hangs on as long as this one, you never know. It might come out someday. Then we'd say some of it got lost while it was hidden, put out a new edition. Lyndushkin's actual words could never be printed of course; they'd conflict with ours. But we wouldn't let any important revelations get buried.'

'And if you don't have control – if the real samizdat reaches someone who won't play ball?'

'We'll cross that bridge when we come to it,' Parritt said complacently.

'The poor bastard,' Keeper murmured. 'He was worried about the wrong gang of censors.'

'You don't like it? Well, you can blame yourself for this part, Keeper. We wouldn't be pushing that book out if we didn't think we need it for self-defence. You're forcing us into it.'

'And the rest, what forced you into that?'

'History.'

There was a pause.

'That had to be it,' Keeper said at last. 'Another golden chance to cut the losses, to make sure we came through no matter what. Another worthy cause.' He glanced over his shoulder at Parritt. 'Is that what Holman decided? Did he put in a P.S., telling me to co-operate for the good of mankind?'

'No, he left that up to you. That was your bargain, wasn't it? You'd be the judge?'

Keeper looked down at the crumpled jacket in the chair by the window.

'You can believe me,' Parritt said.

Keeper started to bend.

'Inside pocket,' Parritt reminded him.

Keeper pulled the .45 from the holster slung over the chair. Straightening up, he turned slowly and pointed the gun at Parritt.

As if he thought Keeper was offering something and was trying to make it out, Parritt cocked his head and peered tentatively into the shadow.

'I ought to kill you,' Keeper said.

The conjugation comforted Parritt, though not enough to move. 'Vengeance, all you see is vengeance. Think of the issues, for God's sake.'

'Survival. Isn't that the issue? Well, I'm thinking beyond that. I'm thinking that by the time you've arranged our precious survival there won't be anything worth saving.'

'It's not a sure thing either way,' Parritt observed. Then he stepped forward and stretched out his hand. 'Come on. You're not going to use that.' He was nearer to the light; his smile could be dimly seen.

It was the smile that did it. Tolerant, bemused, with its hint of secrets, of important business elsewhere that could not be kept waiting.

Keeper's finger contracted on the trigger.

There was the sound, the darkness cracking, and a crash as the force of the bullet rammed Parritt backward into a metal cabinet on the wall. He bounced off, a rubbery bounce like part of an acrobatic routine, and slumped into the desk chair. The wound, the billow of red, clung to his shoulder like a bloody crab. Parritt put his good arm across his chest and fingered the blood, then brought his hand down to look at it. His eyes flickered as if he were going to faint; then, finding Keeper again, they opened wide, held steady. This was the punishment, he realized. There was even a small nod, a signal of acceptance.

But Keeper couldn't stop himself. He took aim once more, very carefully this time. Parritt watched, almost fascinated, gazing at the end of the barrel. Unprepared to accept further punishment, and so unbelieving it would come.

He knew even before he had pulled the trigger. This shot would kill.

Parritt gasped. 'Keeper, are you –'

The shot ended it. The whole front of Parritt's shirt coloured with a red nebula.

There was a scream. And another shot. Keeper spun towards the open door to the outer office, saw Panneau with a gun crouched behind a desk aiming at him. There were moans rising from hidden corners, and a girl's sobbing.

He knew that he wanted to live, only that, and waved the gun in front of him to scare death away. Panneau ducked lower behind the desk, out of sight. Keeper spun and crashed through the french windows. A stinging of glass on his face and hands, then he was running across the lawn, the wet air in his face, sizzling in his hot chest. He heard shooting from behind, but he kept going, heading beyond the reach of light.

Just as a bank of floodlights came on across the lawn, he passed through the gates. His feet pounded ahead until he reached a corner, a busier avenue that intersected the residential street. Then he stopped, suddenly, like a petty thief realizing that what he had stolen would not be missed.

No one came after him.

For five, ten minutes he stood on the corner, wondering where to go. When he had pulled the trigger a second time he had joined an underground; but it was an underground without a base, without a meaning. The revolution entrusted with upholding the principles at stake had already been fought long, long ago. So he stood on the corner, the moment of indecision lengthening to twenty minutes, until very faintly he heard the hee-haw claxon of a police car. Or was it an ambulance? Then he moved off into the night.

He would walk the streets tonight, he thought. Then tomorrow, early, he would go to the airport and claim his son.

More About Penguins and Pelicans

Penguinews, which appears every month, contains details of all the new books issued by Penguins as they are published. From time to time it is supplemented by *Penguins in Print*, which is our complete list of almost 5,000 titles.

A specimen copy of *Penguinews* will be sent to you free on request. Please write to Dept EP, Penguin Books Ltd, Harmondsworth, Middlesex, for your copy.

In the U.S.A.: For a complete list of books available from Penguin in the United States write to Dept CS, Penguin Books Inc., 7110 Ambassador Road, Baltimore, Maryland 21207.

In Canada: For a complete list of books available from Penguin in Canada write to Penguin Books Canada Ltd, 41 Steelcase Road West, Markham, Ontario

Double-Barrel

Nicolas Freeling

A policeman is a bureaucrat. So is a Nazi death camp commandant. Is that why they got on so well together?

They told Inspector Van der Valk to pose as a bureaucrat, go to the dreariest town in Northern Holland and forget he was a policeman. They wanted him and his wife to become small-town eavesdroppers and 'peeping Toms' like everybody else. Just to find out who was writing letters so poisonous that two people committed suicide and everyone was scared of everyone else.

It could have been Van der Valk's dreariest job . . . except that he found out a lot about himself, and his wife, small towns, and just by chance uncovered the worst unpunished war criminal since Eichmann.

and

Because of the Cats

King of the Rainy Country

Love in Amsterdam

Maigret and the Enigmatic Lett

Georges Simenon

Pietr the Lett had for years been clocked across the
European frontiers by Interpol. Who was he, this
international swindler with the skin of a
chameleon? Was he Oswald Oppenheim, friend of
multi-millionaires? Or Olaf Swann, a Norwegian
merchant officer down at Fécamp? Or Fédor
Yurovich, a down-and-out Russian drunk? Or could
he have been the twisted corpse they found on the
Pole Star express when it drew into Paris?

It cost Maigret one of his best inspectors – and a
ducking in the sea – to unravel one of the most
tortuous puzzles of identity he had ever handled.

and

Maigret and the Hundred Gibbets

Maigret at the Crossroads

Maigret Goes Home

Maigret Meets a Milord

Maigret Mystified

Maigret Stonewalled

The Sailors' Rendezvous